Do the Right Thing!

"If nobody did anything, nothing in the world would be different. Not everyone realizes that kids can make a difference too. Some adults think we can't, but we can."

—9-year-old girl talking about volunteering

Check it out . . . hundreds of creative, fun ways to help others and help ourselves. Why not . . .

- **PLANT** a community garden
- **TEACH** adults to read
- **RUN** in a charity race
- **RAISE MONEY** for the library
- **MAKE A VIDEO** teaching people how to use the library
- **VOLUNTEER** at a hospital, nursing home, or museum
- **TUTOR** other kids
- **RAISE PUPPIES TO BECOME LEADER DOGS** for the blind

There's something in these pages for everyone! Discover *your* special talents and become part of The Big Help today!

NICKELODEON®
THE BIG HELP™ BOOK

365 WAYS YOU CAN MAKE A DIFFERENCE by VOLUNTEERING!

Alan Goodman

Illustrated by Fiona Smyth

A MINSTREL® BOOK

PUBLISHED BY POCKET BOOKS

New York   London   Toronto   Sydney   Tokyo   Singapore

A MINSTREL PAPERBACK *Original*

A Minstrel Book published by
POCKET BOOKS, a division of Simon & Schuster Inc.
1230 Avenue of the Americas, New York, NY 10020

ISBN: 0-671-51927-1

First Minstrel Books printing October 1994

10 9 8 7 6 5 4 3 2

A MINSTREL BOOK and colophon are registered trademarks of
Simon & Schuster Inc.

NICKELODEON and THE BIG HELP are trademarks of
Nickelodeon, a programming service of Viacom International Inc.

Cover art and interior illustrations by Fiona Smyth

Text design by Stanley S. Drate/Folio Graphics Co. Inc.

Printed in the U.S.A.

This book is printed on recycled paper

Acknowledgments

This book would not have been possible without the early encouragement and suggestions of Susan Pollack and Patricia Favale of the School Volunteer Program in New York. I owe a debt as well to Chris Fischer of Community Creek Watch, Jill Osofsky of the Yavneh Day School, Elaine Shen of Youth Quest, Karen Seviour of the Horse Rescue Center, Jami Lichtman of the Volunteer Center of San Francisco, and Carole Lam of Self-Help for the Elderly.

Candace Riegelhaupt and Deni Frand at RL&M have been a tremendous source of enthusiasm, advice, and laughs, and I am equally thankful for all three. Melinda Toporoff has been a tireless and resourceful researcher and fact checker in the final hours, and she has my sincere appreciation. Special thanks to Genevieve Kazdin and the KOOL (Kids Only On Line) kids of America Online for your ideas, your commitment, and your stories. To all the kids who spoke to me about your help projects: I have been truly inspired by you, and look forward to seeing you take over the world. Deep affection and gratitude to Albie Hecht for recommending me for this project and for having the guts and determination to make The Big Help a reality; to mom, for her example of a lifetime of selfless service to others; and to my wife, who has helped in at least a hundred ways.

And to the one on the way.

CONTENTS

Introduction   1

How to Start a Group   5

Helping Our Town   10

The Art of Helping   19

Helping Other Kids   28

Help for the Needy   44

Our Planet Needs Help!   57

Helping the Animal Kingdom   78

Staying Healthy, Helping the Sick   91

Help Across the Generations   102

Helping Our World   114

Contents

○ ○

How to Make Your Pennies and Dollars Help   122

The Final Way to Help   129

Our Helpers in The Big Help   131

INTRODUCTION

"Share! Clean! Fix! Visit! Care! Give! Do! HELP!!"

That's the message of The Big Help, Nickelodeon's campaign of kids united in community service and volunteer efforts nationwide.

The Big Help is big in every way: thousands of projects, millions of kids, many millions of hours of unselfish service to others. And how did it all start? With kids themselves!

Even the words, "share, clean, fix . . ." came from kids.

So what does it all mean?

To some people, helping means being generous and sharing what they have. To others, it means rescuing someone in danger, or just making a job easier to do. Sometimes they get asked. But lots of times, it's kids themselves who come up with ways to help.

The Big Help is new, but kids volunteering isn't. Somebody counted how many hours teenagers volunteer each year, and found out if you had to pay for all that work, it would cost over four billion dollars! Now, that's a lot of zeros. And it doesn't even include all the kids who do volunteer work who aren't in their teens yet!

Even with all that volunteering, there's so much more work to do. Look around you. Do empty soft drink cans by the highway bother you? How about homelessness, or the way people mistreat animals?

1

Would you like to help a little kid learn to read, or a friend do better in math?

Those are just some of the ways people get involved to make life better for all of us. This book contains more ideas, and there are many others we had to leave out of it—or you'd need help just to lift it!

How The Big Help works.

If you've never heard of The Big Help, or missed The Big Help television show, here's how it works: Nickelodeon has a special toll-free phone number to call to pledge how many hours you want to volunteer. One of the organizations working with us will help you find a project in your area that needs you, or you can choose an idea from this book or come up with one on your own that you like better.

Then, just pick the time to work off your pledge. That's all there is to it, unless like most kids you get hooked on volunteering and want to keep at it after the telethon is over.

Introduction

ooooooooooooooooooooooooooo

Why volunteer?

Over and over again, kids say the same thing when you ask them why they volunteer. "It makes me feel good," is the answer you hear.

Another thing kids say is, volunteering makes them feel grown up. Plus, there's a nice side benefit: when you are doing something like learning about the environment, or helping other people who have trouble walking by themselves, you can learn a lot about yourself, too.

Where do you go to do it?

While there are all sorts of places you can go to help other people, there's a lot you can do right from home, too. Projects that help birds and other wildlife are great family activities, or you can use your creative writing or art abilities alone, right in your bedroom.

Your school or house of worship is likely to have groups you can join, and in most communities you'll find service organizations—some are beginning to offer activities for younger members like you.

Choosing a project.

The first thing to remember is, you can do volunteer work and still have a good time. So look for something to do that takes advantage of your interests or talents. For instance, if you play little league baseball, you can take some time with the team to clean up the fields where you play. If you're good at art, you can find a pre-school program that needs help supervising the little children.

All kinds of activities exist that let you work alongside your friends and classmates. Since most organized groups get help from kids all over the city or town where you live, the chances are you'll meet new friends who like doing the same things you do.

Get started!

From watching the news or from talking to friends or just by observing the world around you, find something that interests you and make a change.

Anyone who thinks kids can't make a difference in a grown-up world, stand back and watch them. There are millions of kids in the country, and they are powerful! Even the smallest efforts add up to big results, for you, your family, your community or school, and your world.

Ah, but *how* do you get started? Especially if you don't like working alone? Read on!

HOW TO START A GROUP

Kid volunteer groups are in every school and house of worship, and there are probably dozens of places in your town where you can go and work a few hours a week to help others.

So how come you can't find an organization devoted to a project that interests you? What do they expect you to do? Start your own group?

Hey, wait a minute. Why not?

Kids are doing it all over the country, and they are accomplishing incredible goals people never thought possible—except for people who know how powerful kids are when they get together to do something they find important.

Newspapers are full of stories about kids as young as eight, nine, or ten who talked their local governments into building parks for kids, or got the whole community interested in making dinners for people who had lost their jobs and homes. Others have set up hotlines for kids to call when they are being mistreated, or feel tempted to try dangerous drugs or alcohol, and the only person who talks to them is another kid who has faced the same trouble. One group of first and second graders has collected over $50,000 to save acres and acres of tropical rainforest that was about to be cleared and destroyed!

If you feel everybody is ignoring an important issue, take action and dedicate yourself to making a change.

You have to be serious about your issue, and you have to work hard. Of course, nobody said you can't enjoy yourself while you're doing it!

Here are some steps to get you going, keep you going, and help you succeed. Every one of them may not apply to your project, but look them over for ideas.

1. Make a real commitment.
Don't just complain about a problem, or expect someone else to do something about it. Decide that you are the person who is going to be responsible. Talk to your family or friends and tell them you want to work for change.

2. Set a date to get started.
Let's face it, would any of us ever do our homework if teachers didn't tell us when it was due? Set a deadline to start working on your project and stick to it, and you'll be on your way to making a difference. Even if things move slowly at first, you are better off taking small steps than no steps at all.

3. Find friends to work with you.

People are always surprised to find that lots of others agree with them about problems that need fixing. If you talk to your friends at school or on the playground, you are bound to find a lot of them will want to work with you.

4. Set a goal.

Try to find a way to say in one sentence what you want to do. Here's one example: "We, the kids of West-Fourth Street, want the town council to put up a traffic light at Fourth and Main streets so we can cross safely."

5. Make a special plan for accomplishing it.

For instance, to get the traffic light you'll need to go to a town council meeting and ask the council to do the job. But first, it might be a good idea to compile a whole list of accidents or near misses that make you think the light is necessary. Maybe every member of your group has a specific story to tell. You should write your stories out on paper so when you speak to the council, your ideas are organized and your facts clear.

What next? You may need to stage a public protest to voice your concerns or get signatures on a petition or write to the local newspaper.

Whatever you decide to do, list the steps you will need to take and put them into a plan of action.

6. Give everybody a part to play.

Maybe one person is good at organizing, another person brings the supplies, someone else gets parents to drive you where you need to go, a fourth person is good at talking to newspaper reporters . . . you get the idea. If you share the work (and the credit!) you'll get more kids interested, you won't forget to take care of important details, and you'll get more done.

7. Meet regularly.
Depending on the project, you may be able to get started right away, or you may need to plan for weeks. If detailed planning is necessary, make sure you get together on a set day each week or so. Have a goal for each meeting so you keep moving forward. And remember, you'll keep your group together longer if part of your meeting includes a trip to the pizza place or you bring video games to play when the meeting is over.

8. Get the facts you need.
If your project requires research from the library or phone calls to people who have information you need, make sure you get the facts to make your presentation convincing.

9. Ask for help.
Businesses, government, and your neighbors will often be willing to help you accomplish what you are trying to do. In fact, they are often more receptive to kids than to adults. So, ask! You may be surprised at their reaction.

10. Don't get discouraged if people treat you like a kid.
Some adults don't realize that what's important to kids matters just as much as what's important to

adults. Be patient, stick to your plan, and keep working. The best way to get respect is to not give up!

11. Keep track of your experiences, and tell the news.
Local TV coverage or a newspaper story is often a great way to get support for your project. So make sure someone in the group keeps track of dates you met, steps you took, and results you accomplished. And don't forget to invite the power of the press to make your cause famous.

Got it? Then there's nothing left to do but go to work!

MAKING WHERE WE LIVE A NICER PLACE.

You're hot. It's the middle of summer. You've got the whole day ahead of you to spend with your friends. All right! So what are you going to do today? Go swimming? Crank up the hose and spray everybody you know (plus some strangers in their passing cars)? Play baseball or ride bikes?

That's when Dad suggests, how about we drive across town and spend most of the day scraping and painting the house of some woman you never met?

"I wasn't too sure I wanted to go," says Nathaniel Shallenberger, who is ten and lives in Texas. "It gets pretty hot in Houston. There wasn't a cloud in the sky, and you couldn't even hope for rain."

But then there was some talk about a stop at Jack in the Box for lunch. Nathaniel agreed.

What had Nathaniel's dad all fired up about volunteering? He had heard about P.S.I., or Private Sector Initiatives, an organization that gets people from churches, big companies, and civic groups to join together in such projects as helping people find employment, teaching pre-school kids, and house painting.

In Houston, they began painting houses in 1985, mostly for older people who couldn't afford to do it themselves. That first year, P.S.I. volunteers painted six houses. Since then, the number has skyrocketed to 1,660, and in addition to painting, they'll do siding, repair doors and windows, fix locks and steps, and complete other household repair jobs.

But is that work for a kid to do? When Nathaniel and his dad got to the house, they didn't find a lot of other kids Nathaniel's age; only one girl he knew from Sunday school was working at that particular job site, even though scout troops and whole families with kids are common in the program. He did find lots of jobs he could do, however, usually by squeezing into little spots where no one else could work, like the area between the garage and the house that could never support the weight of a grown man or woman.

If the hot sun made working uncomfortable, everyone stopped complaining about it when they saw how well the painting was going. "The woman who lived there kept coming to tell us what a good job we were doing," says Nathaniel. "She was pretty thankful. She came over and complimented me a lot, which was a good thing, because you have to do a lot to keep a kid going."

In about five hours, the crew chipped off the old

11

paint and gave the whole house a new coat in light green, with darker green for the trim. "It gave me a good sense of accomplishment," says Nathaniel, who wants to paint again this year. "It was nice to help someone make her life a little better. We took care of the outside, now she only has to worry about the inside."

There was another benefit, too, "I liked doing stuff not a lot of other kids were doing. It made me feel grown up, like I wasn't spending all my time for me. I did something good, instead of playing Nintendo all day."

CLEAN IT UP:

Many communities sponsor Neighborhood Pride Days, when you can become actively involved in painting and rebuilding neglected homes. Contact your Housing Services department, which may supply the paint, supplies, and sometimes even a free lunch. Private Sector Initiatives (P.S.I.) can be reached at: P.S.I., 4 Houston Center, 1331 Lamar, Suite 570, Houston, TX 77010-3026. You can also get involved with sprucing up the homes of people who need your help through an organization called Christmas in April USA, 1225 Eye Street, Suite 601, Washington, D.C. 20005. If you want to do some really serious work, check out Habitat for Humanity, 121 Habitat Street, Americus, GA 31709-3498. Teams of volunteer workers associated with Habitat actually build homes—whole houses—for people with low incomes.

You'd be surprised how many opportunities exist for you to help right in your own community. Choosing to plant a garden the whole neighborhood can enjoy, raise money for a charity, or help build a baseball diamond is really up to you. And you get to decide whether you'd rather work on your own or with your family or friends.

Here are some suggestions to get you thinking:

On Your Own or With Your Family

1 Paint and help rebuild neglected homes.
Follow Nathaniel's lead. You'll make the whole community feel good about a better-looking neighborhood.

2 Keep your yard neat and tidy. Work with your parents to be the hero of your block.

3 Teach a computer class to adults. At thirteen, Matt Stoner of Phoenix, Arizona, started tutoring concerned parents and senior citizens using the Apple and its finder interface. "I always found the experience very gratifying and it is one reason I'm considering a career in teaching after college."

4 Plant a community garden. Neighbors and friends can make your whole block a place you can look at with pride.

5 Give charity runners a burst of refreshment. So, you're all geared up to take part in the big charity race, except for one thing—you hate running. That's okay, you can still serve from the sidelines. Every race needs people to hand cups of water to thirsty racers, and you can be one of them.

And Here Are Some More:

6 Adopt a monument. Keep it clean, decorated with flowers, and weed free.

7 Plant flowers at town hall. Work with the garden club.

8 Teach at your Sunday school.

9 Be a greeter at functions at the family's house of worship.

○ ○

10 Babysit or play with little kids during services where you pray.

11 Help at charity auctions. Your house of worship needs someone to pass out the numbers to bidders and hold up items for sale.

12 Organize items for a rummage sale.

13 Join the block party action. Help set up and staff a table at your house of worship block party.

14 Give a tie-dying lesson.

15 Be a junior crossing guard.

With Your Friends, Club, or Group

16 Erase graffiti. In Rockland, Massachusetts, a group of kids gave up their school vacations to paint over destructive graffiti that covered bathroom walls. And it wasn't just the "good" kids, either! Talk to your school leaders about projects like this to help you take pride in your school.

17 Reduce gang violence. Even in towns away from big cities, people today often feel the threat of gangs on their playgrounds, on street corners, and in their parks. Sometimes, you can help ease the tension between rival gangs by getting them to meet on the peaceful battlefield of a basketball court. Talk to your local youth commissioner to help organize it and spread the word, but make sure the players know it's kids who made it happen, and why.

18 Pay your respects to fallen soldiers and sailors. Before the Memorial Day ceremony in your town, someone needs to go out and put tiny flags on the graves of veterans and make sure the cemetery looks clean and tidy. Why not your club or group? Talk to the Veterans Committee or ask at town hall how to get involved.

19 Go for the gold. From running races to gymnastics competitions, channel the healthy competitive spirit of all the kids in your area into an Inner City Olympics.

2 0 Build a field of dreams. Wouldn't you like to see little league teams compete on what were once glass-strewn lots? Petition business leaders in your area to pay to replace abandoned properties with baseball diamonds.

2 1 Remake a playground. It takes a lot of work to turn a run-down, unused playground into a place where kids want to hang out. It also takes money for new equipment, and grown-ups to help move and put things together.

And Here Are Some More:

2 2 Weed a public garden.

2 3 Be a helper in the parks department office.

2 4 Supervise recreation classes for the town youth committee.

2 5 Assist at sporting events sponsored by the parks committee.

26 Spruce up and paint the community or youth center.

27 Request traffic lights or stop signs at unsafe corners.

28 Adopt a park.

29 Paint the town's fire hydrants (with the town's permission!).

30 Work with the volunteer fire department on their yearly activities.

31 Clean up a ball court.

32 Learn about, and promote, safe water sports.

33 Paint the park benches.

34 Help decorate the town for national holidays.

35 Operate a booth at a town carnival.

THE ART OF HELPING

HOW TO BE A PART OF THE CULTURAL LIFE OF YOUR COMMUNITY.

Do you like to act in plays? Or play a musical instrument? Is history your thing? How about teaching art to little kids? You can play a big role in your community by giving something of yourself to the culture of your town.

When he was eleven years old, Ben Dobson started volunteering at drama workshops near his home in Spencer, Massachusetts. He worked behind the curtain on everything from lighting, sound, and set painting to coaching young kids in plays and helping with the costumes. He was the only one his age for the first three years, until another kid joined him this year to help. "Yes, sometimes you *do* need help," says Ben, "and someone to talk to."

He says the most rewarding part is knowing he was

19

able to make a successful show that "both parents and kids could have fun producing and watching."

History buff.

Across the country in Newbury Park, California, eleven-year-old Megan Hughes does her part in an entirely different way. While most weekends you can find her at the mall or with her friends rollerblading or playing Carmen Sandiego, one Sunday a month she works as a docent, a volunteer lecturer, at the Stagecoach Inn Museum. It sits along the road between Los Angeles and Ventura, where stagecoach travelers over a hundred years ago used to stop for a rest. Back then, sheep and cattle grazed in the valleys and the only way to get around was by horse or stage. These days, Megan's parents drive her.

"When I was six, my parents brought us here for the first time," says Megan, who likes to visit historical sites with her family, "and I just liked it. I asked my mother if I could try out." At first, the staff at the museum thought Megan was too young but they agreed to train her. Her first time in front of a crowd, Megan was a big hit.

To help tell the story of how people lived and worked in the mid 1800s, Megan wears a long dress like the ones worn by women at the tme the inn was active, and she demonstrates how food was made in the kitchen and served in the dining room.

Bringing history to life.

"I act it out," says Megan. She points out the old-fashioned pot-bellied stove, and explains how people had to wait for the ice man to come once a week, since homes had no electricity or refrigerators. "Mostly, I try to tell people that life was a lot harder," she says.

Megan's interests may be historical, but her future plans are entirely modern. In fact, both she and Ben Dobson share a dream: to become television anchor-people.

"I think I may become a television news broadcaster," says Ben. "I was already invited to the CNN News Center in Atlanta for a private tour, with a possible job opening for when I turn eighteen. At the very least, I hope to work behind the scenes with a TV news show."

Megan, whose favorite anchorwoman is the fictional character Murphy Brown, may find the five or six shows she does each day at the museum will give her the solid stand-up experience every reporter needs.

What's your talent?

Whether you like being in front of a crowd or prefer the action behind the scenes, there are many opportunities to make your presence felt in your community. Most local art institutions, libraries, drama groups, and historical or preservation societies have very little money to pay the people who work there and depend

DO YOUR PART:

> If you are into live theater, look for ads or announcements in your local newspaper about current productions. Call the ticket reservation number to tell them you want to volunteer on future productions. If you would like to give tours and demonstrations at a local museum, ask if they have a junior docent program for kids your age. If not, do what Megan Hughes did, ask them to start one anyway!

on volunteers to stretch the budget. That's where you come in.

The following ideas should get you rolling.

On Your Own or With Your Family

36 37 Ben Dobson and Megan Hughes are two examples of how you can participate in the arts near your home, Ben behind the scenes getting the show in front of an audience, and Megan center stage. Look for community theater groups that need assistance, or a museum that has a junior docent program.

38 Give a lecture. Do you know a lot about snakes? Photography? How a jet engine works? Schedule a talk at your local library.

39 Make the library your stage. If you play an instrument, sing, twirl, or dance, the library is a great place to share your talents with the community. Talk to the librarian about cultural programs you can join.

40 Teach adults to read. Reading may seem easy to you, but too many adults in America can't get good jobs because they had to leave school, or for some other reason never got good at reading. Through your guidance counselor, or a local literacy project, you may have the opportunity to work one on one with an adult who really wants to learn.

41 Create a library in your home. It's a good bet that all the families on your block have books they don't want, but don't want to throw away. Consider starting a local library in a spare room or basement, where neighbors can share the books you've collected.

42 Preserve our history at sea. If you live near a maritime or seaport museum, join the volunteers who climb aboard the beautiful ships to clean, paint, and repair them.

43 Donate old videotapes to the library. Remember, since the library is free, you'll be able to borrow them back!

44 Join the library's summer reading program for little kids. Become a reading partner with someone who is just learning reading skills.

45 Make a coloring book. If you are good at art, draw pictures you can bind into a book for a younger kid to color. You can make the book about a child's favorite subject, about the history of your town, or somebody famous you admire. If you want to get your book to lots of kids, ask your librarian to help you find a place to make copies.

And Here Are Some More:

46 Assist at the library. They may need you to run the copying machine, help clean up after visitors leave, or shelve books.

47 Donate a book. If you're done with it, give someone else a chance to borrow it from your library.

48 Help with office work for your town's arts council.

49 Join the village band.

50 Start a photography club.

51 Be a demonstrator in the library's computer center.

52 Be a host family for visiting performers.

53 Be an usher at a concert or event.

With Your Friends, Club, or Group

54 Start a kids' page at your local newspaper. What are your classmates' opinions of the news? Do they agree with the President? Do they worry about war or too much violence? How much TV do they watch each day, and who are their favorite celebrities? Talk to the editor of your local newspaper about starting a page that's just for kids, with an editorial board including you and some of your friends. Get to the heart of how kids feel about events in the world.

55 Save the school music program. Parents and kids in one school district were faced with a problem. Budget cuts forced the school to cancel music lessons, but everyone who cared participated in car washes and yard sales to keep it going. By working together, they raised enough money to keep the music playing.

5 6 Have a Halloween window-painting contest. Talk to the Chamber of Commerce about getting store owners to let you use their windows.

5 7 Celebrate other cultures. For instance, you can have a Fiesta Day—celebrate the cultures of Mexico, Central America, and South America by sampling the food, duplicating the art, and learning about the way natives lived before Columbus arrived.

And Here Are Some More:

5 8 Make posters for the library. How many ways can you say ''Read'' in pictures and words?

59 Throw a pajama party—for little readers.
Okay, we admit it. This one is a little crazy. Publicize a special night of stories, songs, and games for little kids, and hold it at the library. Everybody should come in pajamas—even you!

60 Sponsor a book sale. Collect used books from neighbors and sell them at a discount. The library uses the money to buy new books.

61 Get store owners to display your art class masterpieces.

62 Make a video for the library. Choose a subject like the history of your town or the life of a famous person who lived there. Write the show, borrow a camcorder, and shoot it yourselves.

63 Decorate a wall or bridge underpass with an original mural (but get permission first!)

64 Have a community dance.

65 Sponsor a poetry or essay contest about the town.

66 Give a martial arts demonstration at your youth center.

67 Make banners or flags for town events.

HOW TO MAKE A DIFFERENCE FOR KID JUST LIKE YOU.

"I was born in this country, but I went to a Chinese school and mainly spoke Chinese. I had a lot of trouble with English, but I finally learned it. So when I work with other students on their reading and comprehension, I feel like I can really help a lot, because I used to be like that,"
— Arick Rangwalla, twelve.

"Since math is my best subject, I thought I'd try tutoring in that. Having one person who can answer all your questions is very helpful. You don't have to worry about feeling stupid in front of the whole class."
— Stephen Feyer, thirteen.

"The person I tutored daydreamed a lot. She wasn't excited by school, and didn't have a posi- tive attitude about her work. I really wanted her

*to do better. One night I stayed up until 10:00
trying to think of some way to get through to her.
It used to really bother me.''*
— Sara McKinley, thirteen.

There's good news, and still more good news, about
what happens when you help another kid with a problem. The good news is, you can really make the other
kid's life a little better. And the other good news is,
even if it you don't reach your goal completely, you
can learn something about what it feels like to be
responsible for somebody else.

Arick, Stephen, and Sara all go to school in San
Francisco, and their schools require some volunteer
service. Arick found his tutoring assignment through
Youth Quest, an organization that matches kids with a
variety of volunteer jobs. Stephen and Sara found
their projects through Summerbridge Prep, the junior
version of a national education program called Summerbridge.

How it feels.

For Arick, giving up his Saturday mornings every
other week isn't much of a burden, and he likes the
feeling of helping other kids, especially the foreign-
born students who are having the same difficulty with
the language he had.

"Mostly, I help out when the teacher is busy with
other students. I help them with their spelling, correct
their grammar, and teach them how to say and write
things. I don't do it alone. There are seven or eight
kids like me each time I go.

29

"I figure, if I can help them go from a bad student to a pretty good one, that's good."

Teaching the proper method.

The boy Stephen helped was a grade below him and struggling with fractions. Stephen asked the boy to show him his methods, and Stephen noticed he was making the same mistake over and over. Stephen corrected the problem, showed him some short cuts, and helped him learn his multiplication tables.

One day, Stephen came home and told his mother he wasn't sure how much longer he'd have to tutor the other boy, because that week he got an A.

But then, on the other hand . . .

"I think I worked ten times harder than the other girl did," says Sara McKinley of the student she tutored. "She didn't really return my enthusiasm. She raised her grade a little bit, and that was very rewarding. But I wanted her to do better.

"I want to be a teacher when I grow up, and now I have more respect for teachers and what they go through every day. I guess you learn a lot even if you're not the one learning the concepts."

No experience necessary.

All over the country, kids are finding out how easy it is to work with other school kids, and how rewarding. In the New York City School Volunteer Program you don't have to be some whiz kid to be a tutor. The only requirement is that you can read at least three grade levels above the person you are tutoring, and School Volunteer Program employees train you how to do the rest. The program starts with Reading Buddies—fifth and sixth graders who help second graders read books—and continues all the way into high-school years.

SHARE your education:

The Volunteer Center of San Francisco, (415) 982-8999, publishes a guide to youth volunteer opportunities with close to 200 agencies and organizations that welcome your help. Among them is Youth Quest, the Saturday community service program for 7th and 8th graders formed so kids who would normally be considered too young could work with an adult supervisor in projects. To reach them, call the same number: (415) 982-8999. Summerbridge and Summerbridge Prep assign volunteer tutors to younger students needing help one afternoon a week. Summerbridge's phone number is (415) 931-2422. The New York City School Volunteer Program is at (212) 213-3370. In other parts of the country, talk to your guidance counselor, teacher, or librarian about becoming a tutor or school volunteer.

Of course, teaching other kids what you know isn't the only way to help them. There are kids with physical challenges that can use a boost from you. Other kids may be victims of violence and abuse and just need a friend.

Take a look at this long list of different help projects, and find a project that interests you.

On Your Own or With Your Family

68 Teach another kid what you know. Like Arick, Stephen, and Sara, you can be a peer tutor for a student who needs extra help. You don't have to be the smartest kid in the class to help someone else, in fact, a lot of the best tutors are kids who used to need help themselves.

69 "This year, I worked at the Discovery Museum. It's basically a place with fun activities for kids, with exhibits about animals, science, a computer lab. There's a carrousel for them to ride that we power by pedaling like a bicycle. We paint their faces, and just help in any way. Mostly, I just like being around the little kids. They're just really cute.'' Nathan Wilson, twelve, San Francisco.

70 Be a hero on two wheels. If you're good with tools and can fix bikes, try finding cheap bicycles at yard sales to repair and give away to kids who can't afford them.

71 Make a book of your own. If you have a computer at home and a program to do desk-

top publishing, why not write and illustrate a simple book for a little kid to read? You can make it a story about the child—even put in his or her name!

7 2 **"I volunteer for the Arizona State PTA.** I just got back from the state convention, where we had our second annual Youth Day, in which I helped to make sure [things] were running smoothly. . . . I also worked as a page for the PTA general meeting, and ran a scholarship fund auction booth for hours at a time. It is a lot of fun, and you know you are working for a real good cause." Charlie Pabst, fourteen, Glendale, Arizona.

7 3 **Help a young kid learn to love music.** If you play an instrument other kids can try, arrange to give a group of really young kids a chance to play it. It can be the first step they take toward playing an instrument themselves.

7 4 **Raise dogs for the blind or physically challenged.** Dogs can be trained to help people do the things they can't do themselves, but before the dogs go into the training program, they need families like yours to raise them. Contact Leader Dogs for the Blind, 1039 South Rochester Road, Rochester, MI 48307, (313) 651-9011, to offer your home for the puppies they provide.

7 5 Invent a product to help a friend. From *Nick News:* Twelve-year-old Josh Parsons wanted to help his friend David Potter, thirteen, who was unable to throw a ball after losing his hands in an accident when he was four. The glove Josh created was a tremendous success. He patented the design, and has made a second glove free of charge for another kid who needed one. ''I just thought about it and made a design,'' Josh says.

7 6 Work in an after-school program. Young kids sometimes need a place to play until their parents finish work, and they also need someone to supervise them. Talk with a teacher or your council person about how to set up a center for kids if your town doesn't already have one.

7 7 Train special athletes. If you have a special talent for athletics, talk to your school coach or phys ed teacher about working with athletes who have physical or mental challenges, but still want to play sports. In some areas, special training is available for young coaches who want to volunteer.

7 8 Teach a kid with mental challenges to ride a horse. People who work with kids who have mental obstacles find riding a horse helps their coordination, confidence, and self-esteem. It's called therapeutic riding, and there are ranches all over the country where you can participate.

7 9 Call "Kid Company." "Kid Company" is a radio program broadcast on WBZ-AM 1030 in Boston, Saturdays from 5 to 7 PM EST. The show features live guests, prizes, celebrities, news for kids, and live discussions. Make your voice heard! (617) 254-1030.

8 0 Join the chat on an online service. Spread the word about your interests, projects, and ideas on computer boards with special-interest areas for kids. Be careful! Depending on the service you use, charges can mount up.

And Here Are Some More:

8 1 Be a friend to abused children. Centers for children who have been victims of abuse need volunteers your age to help play with the kids and read to them.

8 2 Help mothers at a shelter for battered women. Take care of the children while their mothers study or look for work.

8 3 Walk in the March of Dimes. The money you raise by getting sponsors to pay for the miles you walk goes toward finding cures for childhood diseases.

8 4 Turn an enemy into a friend. Go out of your way to patch up differences with someone you know.

8 5 Help physically challenged kids with art projects.

8 6 Help out at a camp for the blind and visually impaired.

8 7 Teach a photography class at the Y or community center.

8 8 Babysit for a younger brother or sister.

89 Volunteer for student council and school government committees.

90 Lead a blind kid from class to class.

91 Be a hall monitor.

92 Teach a friend to rollerblade.

With Your Friends, Club, or Group

93 Become part of a support team for other kids. At age twelve, Gege Campbell of Long Island, New York, joined HUGS, or Human Understanding and Growth Seminars, a group that sponsors weekend seminars throughout the year to train kids in how to deal with crises. "We talk about suicide, grief, eating disorders, but also about humor, human differences, and how young people can support each other," she says. "You learn how to work together as a group and gain the resources to deal with your problems." Teen institutes like HUGS exist in many states throughout the country, but you can work with your guidance counselor to start one.

94 Record books for the blind. Matthew (ten) and Jonathan (twelve) Michels are brothers who were among the youngest people ever to record a book so that blind kids could listen to the story. "We went to this place in New York, Recording for the Blind, with our scout troop," says Matthew. They broke into two groups and recorded two different books, with all of the boys playing different parts. Matthew, who loves mysteries and science fiction, says he liked reading a book that was one of his favorites when his mother read to him at night. "I shared that mystery with them. It was like I was reading it to them." And Jonathan remembers talking about how they were "doing something good and helping other people." The best part? "Talking to the other guys after it was over, and laughing about all the mistakes we made until we got it right." Contact Recording for the Blind for details. Recording for the Blind, 545 Fifth Avenue, New York, NY 10017; (212) 557-5720.

7 5 Start a Natural Helpers club. "The program is run through our school to help kids through tough times. The Natural Helpers are there for kids to listen and possibly help them through a bad situation, or to help them figure things out. Natural Helpers go to a camp for two or three days to learn ways of helping kids without telling them what to do. If a child has a problem with another child then we would arrange a meeting for them to discuss what is wrong in front of one of the Natural Helpers in case they need help explaining things. The best thing about being a Natural Helper is when you are helping a person and you see that they feel better when you are done than when you first started talking to them. You see the relief on their face and you know you have helped someone through a problem you may have had once yourself." Megan Rogers, fourteen, Escondido, California.

9 6 Join a help group for kids with a parent who has cancer. From *Nick News:* When Jon Wagner Holtz, twelve, found out his mother had cancer, he felt he needed to talk to other kids who would understand what he was going through. He started the Komen Kids support group, now in five cities. "It's helpful knowing that they're going through the same thing and that I'm not alone," says Joshua Berk, thirteen.

9 7 Write to young shooting victims. Kids in the Supplemental Program for Educational Skills in Roxbury, Massachusetts, know how hard it can be to grow up in a tough neighborhood. One of the best ways to turn your back on crime and hatred is to connect with other kids, so they send letters to cheer up kids who have gotten in trouble with gangs.

9 8 Help track down missing kids. Police across the country believe they can find kids easier if they have fingerprints on file to help trace the kids. You can get involved by talking to your local police about setting up a table at the mall, at fairs, or at your school where fingerprints can be taken.

9 9 Join Kids Against Crime. Founded in 1985 by a twelve-year-old, this organization teaches crime prevention and how to keep from being the victim of a crime. It also sponsors a hotline staffed by kids who are trained to help young callers. Their address is Kids Against Crime, P.O. Box 22004, San Bernardino, CA 92406. Their phone number is (909) 882-1344.

100 Form a chapter of Middle School S.A.D.D.

Middle school kids can join Students Against Drunk Driving's program called I'm Special Because I'm Me, which deals with learning how illegal drugs can mess up your health and your life. Write to them at P.O. box 800, 255 Main Street, 3rd Floor, Marlboro, MA 01752.

101 Put on an information fair for kids home alone.

There's a lot to learn about being safe at home when you're waiting for your parents to finish work, or if you find yourself alone. Your local police, fire department, and phone company can give you all the details on what to do in case of an emergency or if you get scared.

102 Learn sign language.

You'll find a whole new group of friends who are hearing-impaired if you learn the international sign language they speak with their hands.

103 Learn what to do if someone tries to hurt you.

Most of us will never have to worry about it, but there are people in the world who try to hurt kids. Talk to your guidance counselor about doing an assembly where police officers can educate you about the dangers to avoid.

1 0 4 Sponsor a toy repair clinic. Lots of toys are stuffed away in basement boxes because they are missing a wheel, or a leg mysteriously ripped off the body. Sometimes a hand tool, a needle and thread, some glue, or nontoxic paint is all it takes to make the toy almost as good as new. Get the neighborhood parents together with their repair kits, then have everyone bring their broken toys. Hey, how about this: you can donate any repaired toys you've outgrown to an orphanage or children's hospital.

1 0 5 Give special kids a chance to enjoy your town's carnival or fair. Do the firemen or Jaycees in your town sponsor an annual fund-raising fair? Talk to them about setting aside a day for kids with physical and mental challenges. Volunteers provide one-on-one pairing with children who have special needs during the Conejo Valley Days carnival in Thousand Oaks, California. The kids get a private, advance opportunity to enjoy the rides and games before the yearly carnival opens to the public. Called Special Kids Day, it's been a success for over ten years now.

1 0 6 Stock a lake with trout for physically challenged kids to catch. In Sacramento, Kids Catch a Smile Day gives them a chance to fish, eat hot dogs, sing songs, and win prizes.

107 Form a youth soccer team. The hottest sport around for kids gives you something to do after school.

108 Start a youth court. Help resolve problems between kids by letting them argue their cases in front of a jury of kids. Talk to your guidance counselor about setting up a court that is fair.

And Here Are Some More:

109 Participate in the annual holiday toy drive.

110 Get your town to start a hotline for kids who need to talk to someone when they feel troubled.

111 Offer your club members as Special Olympics helpers.

112 Throw a party (Halloween, Christmas, etc.) for kids with special needs.

113 Go bowling or square dancing with kids who have mental challenges.

114 Put pressure on town officials to get wheelchair ramps at public places like the post office, town hall, the mall, and the movie theater.

115 **S**ponsor and promote lifesaving classes from the Red Cross.

116 **W**rap holiday gifts for the children of prison inmates.

SHARe

WHAT KIDS CAN DO TO AID THE HOMELESS
AND HUNGRY

How many times have you stood in front of the open refrigerator, staring into it and feeling as if there's nothing to eat?

Imagine it were true. Imagine really having nothing to eat. Not a can of soup. Not a cookie. Nothing at all.

"The people who come into C.A.S.T. are like that," says Alex Williams, a thirteen-year-old from Greenport, New York. She began helping at Community Action for Southold Town (C.A.S.T.) when she was eleven. "They could be on welfare, or just really poor. They can be pretty desperate."

C.A.S.T. becomes an emergency safety net for them, providing some necessities for a few days until they get back on their feet. Adults who work there will also help them get heat for their homes, housing, job placement, and other essentials. At holiday time, there

44

are usually some donated gifts to distribute, too, and that's how Alex got involved.

"I went there with my mom to help arrange it," she remembers. "We laid the gifts out on tables, and people could come in and get a few items. I felt really sad about it."

Volunteers needed.

Because the people in the C.A.S.T. office are so busy, they hardly have time to go through everything that is donated. So from time to time, Alex and her mom go into the C.A.S.T. basement, where goods are stored. One time, her scout troop came along to help organize the basement.

"People just drop off cans of food, cereal and other stuff in boxes and bags, and its kind of all over the place. Sometimes the food is expired, so we take that out. We put everything on shelves, and try to make it look like a store. At Christmas time, we decorate it so it's a little nicer," says Alex.

Going through the items one by one has given her a lesson in what sorts of things people give to charity, and she has a few ideas of her own about what might be more appropriate.

Give basic items.

"People give a lot of food you wouldn't use," she says, "like a can of clam sauce. It's one of the last things you would need! They should give more things like baby formula or baby food, things like that, and cut down on the canned vegetables that are out of date. You've got to think, they're people too, and if it'll hurt you, it'll hurt them just as much.'' Alex also wishes the people could choose from a greater variety of items. "There should be more cans of vegetable soup, which is hearty, and fewer cans of tomato.''

Even though it's depressing to think about people needing so much help, Alex says she enjoys what she does at C.A.S.T. and even finds it fun to do. "I like doing it,'' she says. "It's really fun. You know you're helping people out.''

What takes you just a couple of hours every few

GIVE YOUR TIME:

Community service groups and food pantries like C.A.S.T. need donations, but they also need people to help organize the gifts and keep the place tidy. Ask at your house of worship or school guidance counselor how to find a group where you can help.

months can make an important change in someone else's life. Other good deeds, like planting and tending a community garden meant for feeding poor people, can bring the whole neighborhood together on a project.

Look for one on this list that looks good to you.

On Your Own or With Your Family

117 Sponsor a kid at the Y. Give someone else a chance to enjoy the activities at your Y by raising the money for his or her membership.

118 Collect deposit cans and donate the money. Would most people really miss the money they get back from soft drink can deposits? But put all those nickels and dimes together, and you can make quite a contribution to a homeless shelter or fund.

119 Distribute blankets, pillows, and clothing to the homeless. Ask your neighbors to check the attic for bedding and clothing they no longer use.

120 Clip coupons. Save the coupons your family doesn't use and arrange them in folders according to categories: food, household items, etc. Leave the coupons at your local food pantry. Every so often, drop by and discard any coupons that are expired.

121 Sponsor a mitten and scarf drive. When it's cold outside, homeless people will appreciate the kindness of mittens and scarves from people who have purchased inexpensive mittens or knitted them themselves.

122 Trick-or-treat for food. Sure, candy is food, but we're talking about the kind of food that can keep a hungry family going. Instead of chocolate and sweets, ask for canned goods and grains, then deliver them to a shelter or food bank for people who can't afford dinner, let alone a new Halloween costume.

123 Raid the attic for old toys. Most of us have toys we haven't touched in years. But lots of kids don't have any toys at all. Fill a box with the ones you'll never miss and take them over to a homeless shelter, or a center for mothers and kids who had to leave home.

○ ○

124 Donate old books. Kids at the homeless shelter will appreciate books you've already finished reading.

125 Give away clothes you can't wear. If it doesn't fit anymore, what's it doing cluttering your drawers? Go through your clothes with your parents and try to find some stuff to give to kids who need it.

126 Give kitchen appliances to food banks. If your parents buy a new coffee maker or pots and pans, encourage them to donate the old ones to a food bank.

And Here Are Some More:

127 Make drawings and decorations for shelters.

128 Start a learning center for needy kids.

129 Work in a thrift store.

130 Call the fire department to get fire hydrant sprinkler caps so kids in the neighborhood can cool off without reducing the water pressure.

131 Have a poster contest to raise awareness about homelessness.

132 Read stories to kids in shelters.

133 Give old sports equipment to a family that can't afford new things.

134 Help at the front desk at a drop-in center.

135 Bring a pot of flowers to a residential facility.

136 Bake cookies for residents at a shelter.

137 Make a back-to-school box with school supplies and clothes you've outgrown for a kid in a homeless center.

138 Make Easter baskets for a residential facility.

139 Make a first-aid kit for a homeless shelter.

140 Raise money to pay for vaccinations for kids whose parents can't afford health care.

141 Open up your country home to a kid from the city.

○ ○

142 **T**ake your video game player and some favorite cartridges to a homeless center for an afternoon.

With Your Friends, Club, or Group

143 **"I** worked at homeless shelters preparing food—chicken, salad, sandwiches, cookies, Jell-O. There were eight kids, three in the kitchen cooking and the rest serving. At first I was kind of scared being around homeless people. I thought, I don't know these people. But when we were done, they all said we did a good job. The next time we went, they all waved to us as we came in. Working with the other kids was fun. It was important that we all did our parts. If one person was missing, it messed everything up. We were from different schools, and some of us have kept in touch. Actually being with the homeless people and getting to know them, I learned not to be afraid. I felt like I was helping people that needed help." Brandy Fontenot, fourteen, San Francisco.

144 **S**ponsor a food drive. With permission from a local supermarket, kids can collect big cartons of food for hungry people by asking shoppers to buy a few extra items they won't use and toss them in your box. The items—canned foods, boxes of rice and pasta, baby foods, and other stuff that won't spoil—work best.

145 "**My Faith Builders group at church collected Turkey Bucks.** That's this thing where every year at Thanksgiving, the supermarket hands out coupons when you buy a lot of food. You can save them up and get the turkey cheaper. So we announced it every other week at church, and when we had enough we went down to the store and cashed them in. We got seven or eight turkeys. Then, we gave very poor people these humongous turkeys. I felt happy we were giving poor people all this stuff and we were being generous to them. It's also fun when lots of kids come together like that. If there's only one kid, it doesn't work."—Benjamin Shallenberger, seven, Houston.

146 **Collect Christmas gifts for kids.** From *Nick News:* In Berkeley, California, S.A.Y.-Y.A.Y. (Save American Youth-Youth Advocates for Youth) was started by kids to collect toys for homeless children. "I personally want everyone to have a home. I want peace in the world, but I know that's basically impossible but you can still hope for it, hope for anything,'' says one eleven-year-old member who is a former homeless child herself.

147 A new way to feed the hungry—plant them a garden. In a once-vacant field at Peoria Street and Garfield Boulevard on Chicago's South Side, a small garden patch provides luscious canta-loupes, strawberries, broccoli, and spinach for hungry neighborhood residents. Seeds, soil, and assistance come from Green Chicago, a program of the Chicago Botanic Garden and St. Basil-Visitation Parish, but kids as young as nine are busy weeding, planting, and picking. Volunteers in over twenty-five similar gardens in Chicago are beautifying communities and filling bellies, in a program that's been active for more than eleven years.

148 Pick oranges and grapefruits. All over Los Angeles, tucked away in people's private yards and on the grounds of big companies, are the remains of the giant orange and grapefruit groves that used to cover the area. Most of that fruit was never picked, and was left to rot and fall to the ground, until

Rhapsody in Green was formed. The environmental group restores damaged areas by planting the right trees and native grasses, but one of their most interesting projects is sending volunteers of all ages into the fields to pick fruit that would go to waste and deliver it to regional food banks. Last year, the volunteers, from kids to senior citizens, picked about 100,000 pounds of fruit. "When kids are not in the field picking fruit with adults, side by side, they are seeing a world that is sane," says one of Rhapsody in Green's founders, Jon Earl. (213) 654-5821.

149 Does your mall have a wishing well or fountain? Does the money go to charity? Find out, and offer to have your group wrap all the coins and make the donations yourself.

150 Display the photos of Shooting Back. Homeless kids were given cameras to use to document their world. You can see things through their eyes by getting this unique photo exhibit for your school to display. Write for information to Shooting Back, 1901 18th Street NW, Washington, DC 20009. Their phone number is (202) 232-5169.

151 What happens to the uneaten food from your school cafeteria? We're not talking about what you leave on your plate. We mean the good food left in the kitchen. Talk to school officials about donating it to a shelter or soup kitchen. Then . . .

152 Collect uneaten food from institutions and businesses. Restaurants and businesses

that serve food to their employees frequently throw
out what they can't use, but with your prodding,
they can get it to hungry people who are grateful for
the leftovers.

And Here Are Some More:

153 Perform a puppet show for kids at a center for battered women and children.

154 Invite a less-fortunate kid to play basketball or other after-school activity.

155 Donate art supplies for kids who are homeless.

156 Fill a food basket for a food pantry.

157 Create a "wish list" team for kids in shelters and recreational programs. Dedicate your group to providing things kids need on a case-by-case basis.

158 Collect unused makeup, perfume, fancy soaps, and other small luxuries for a shelter for abused women.

159 Decorate a homeless shelter for the holidays.

160 Have a "canned food instead of gifts" birthday party.

161 Help paint a residential facility.

Give

HOW KIDS CAN KEEP THE ENVIRONMENT SAFE FOR PLANTS, ANIMALS, AND OURSELVES.

If you looked at the narrow creek that flows near Oka Road in Los Gatos, California, you probably wouldn't think it's much different from any other creek its size.

But you'd be wrong. What's special about Los Gatos Creek is that it flows right by the Yavneh Day School, where second graders use the creek to conduct experiments. They keep such detailed records about the life of the stream and the pond that feeds it that they probably know more about it than any scientist.

For two years, the students have taken measurements of the water and its chemistry. The kids also observe the plant and animal life and keep charts and graphs that describe what they find there.

What do they do?

"We measure the velocity," says Marisa Witkin, who is seven years old. "We stand five feet from a net and put a cork in the water. When the net catches the cork, it tells how fast the creek is flowing."

"We also test the water's pH," says Marisa. That's the measurement that tells them whether the water is too acidic or too alkaline to keep plants and animals alive. They take the water's temperature in three places: on the surface of the water, where it's deepest, and in the middle. If they see any bugs, fish, tadpoles, frogs, or crayfish, they write that down, too.

Back in the classroom, the kids do experiments with their teacher, Jill Osofsky, to see how the fertilizer we put on our lawns and the bait we use to kill snails can poison the water in creeks.

Young scientists.

By keeping track of what's happening to the creek and pond, the kids are doing just what scientists do to learn how the water and life within it change from season to season. They may also be the first to know whether people are doing things to pollute the water.

Studying the little creek next to their school has gotten the kids interested in all the waterways in the area. "We wrote a letter to the mayor and the city council," says Eli Berkowitz, who is eight, "asking them to protect creeks, streams, and lakes." Recently, some highway construction in the county forced workmen to divert a portion of the creek, and at a ceremony to dedicate the new stretch of creek, the kids from Yavneh planted a tree and sang a song in front of all the adults who came to watch.

Eli says he's not sure yet, but someday he might like a job doing the kind of work he's learning now. But while he's still in school, he'll continue studying Los Gatos Creek with his friends, assuming they can find a new bucket.

"Last time we went down there," he says, "I was trying to catch some water and bugs in a bucket, and the water was so strong it carried the bucket away!" If anybody finds a bucket in a creek in the Santa Clara Valley, you'll know whose it is!

The first step.

Monitoring the condition of the stream by your school is the kind of project that will make more people aware of environmental perils. You'll find more kids are suddenly interested in protecting the earth's resources, as well as cleaning up what's been destroyed so far.

Whether you do it as part of a large group, or you just take a couple of hours on your own to fish trash and debris out of a nearby lake or stream, cleaning up the environment might be the second-most-important volunteer activity you can perform.

The most important? Probably protecting the environment before it gets even more polluted than it is now.

Because of waste and misuse, our waterways and forests are in terrible trouble. But it doesn't stop there. Every time someone is careless about our natural resources, it ends up affecting the animals that use those resources—including animals like us!

Down the drain.

You might be shocked to learn that every one of us uses an average of 150 gallons of water every day! That's for drinking, cooking, washing, and flushing, and doesn't even count the water that gets used to grow our food or to manufacture the things we buy. Already, too much of the water available to us is too dirty to be safely used. There's none to waste.

Conservation doesn't end with watching water use. Anytime someone in your house leaves on a light or TV when no one is using it, they are wasting resources, too. Think of the oil, coal, or nuclear fuel they burn to create that electricity (and remember, all that energy production creates pollution that goes into the air, the ground, and the water) and you may think twice about leaving a room lit up when no one's inside. You can probably come up with plenty of other

examples of how waste is using up our planet's limited raw materials.

Take it back!

Recycling is another way we can protect our environment every day, and kids probably know it more than adults do. Kids are growing up with recycling bins in their school cafeterias, something their parents never saw when they were young. While it's important to be patient with adults who are still learning, there's really no excuse anymore not to buy products made from recycled aluminum, glass, plastic, and paper, and certainly no reason not to recycle everything we possibly can.

Kids who get involved with doing good for the environment are lucky. In most cases, they get to see the results of their efforts right away. Some kids are even learning important facts about science and nature that may turn into the work they do the rest of their lives.

If you can't find a group to join in your area, the

following list includes plenty of ideas to get you started.

IF YOU **CARE:**

A ctive environmental groups that welcome kids are in every community. One of the more prominent national ones is the Izaak Walton League of America, which sponsors Save Our Streams. Their address is 1401 Wilson Blvd., Level B, Arlington, Va 22209. Ask for the kids brochure on saving our streams. You can also contact Global ReLeaf, part of the group American Forest. Their focus is on replanting forests that have been chopped down and not replaced. Write them at P.O. Box 2000, Washington, DC 20013. Their phone number is (202) 667-3300. If you want more information about recycling, write to The Environmental Defense Fund, 257 Park Ave. So., New York, NY 10010. Youth Service America (their address is in the back of the book) can give you information about groups in your area that are interested in saving the environment.

On Your Own, or With Your Family

162 Don't litter. As incredible as it seems, people still drop candy wrappers, empty cans, and other waste in the road, on the sidewalk, in the woods, and in the lakes. But not you. Right? When you go hiking or boating, take along a litter bag for your stuff, and whatever else you find.

163 Be the family recycler. Hey, it's not nearly as messy as cleaning the bathrooms! First, find out what the recycling regulations are in your community. (In some towns, you need to separate newspapers from magazines, for instance, and in others they can be bundled together.) Then, choose a spot in the garage or basement where you can line up boxes to sort aluminum cans, plastic, and different-colored glass. Make sure anything that contained food or beverages is carefully rinsed so you don't attract bugs. On recycling day, you need to place your bins at the curb if your town does house-to-house pick-up, or ride with your folks to the recycling center for disposal. If the bins and paper feel a little heavy, just imagine if every family dumped that much stuff into the ground!

164 Help sort recyclables. Even if you collect containers to recycle at home and school, that doesn't mean the job is done! Your recycling center may need help sorting items, cleaning areas, and helping people with drop-offs.

○ ○

165 Elect a family "energy watchdog." Is there someone in the house who always leaves on lights and TVs? Maybe you need an energy watchdog to remind that person about conservation. You can also get professional help to find where your family is wasting energy. In some towns, the electric company will send a representative to your home to show you where insulation, weather stripping around doors, and other inexpensive repairs can make a big difference in the cost and waste of the power you use. Talk to your parents about taking a good look at how your family uses energy.

166 Plant a tree. When we burn coal, oil, and other fuels, a dangerous gas (carbon dioxide) is produced. The gas gets trapped in our atmosphere and blocks the sun's heat from escaping back into space. Many scientists believe those gasses will eventually warm our planet enough to kill many animal species. We need to cut down on the energy we use, but another help is planting more trees. Trees and other plants use carbon dioxide gas to grow. With your parents' help, choose a spot around your yard to plant a few young trees from the garden store. Then, watch them grow year after year. You'll be helping the planet for many years to come.

167 Clean the beach or riverbed. State beaches need help bagging litter that collects throughout the summer season. And keeping riverbeds clear of trash is a yearlong need.

168 Boycott plastic foam. Styrofoam—often used to make throw-away hot drink cups and take-out containers—is an environmental mess. It is made with chemicals that may destroy the ozone layer, a dome of gas that protects the earth from getting too much sun. And besides, once you throw it away it will never decompose, or return to the earth. It just stays Styrofoam forever. If you must use take-out containers or disposables, look for those made of paper instead of plastic.

169 Care for plants. Learn how to care for plants and flowers around your yard and keep them thriving naturally. If you use fertilizers, look for brands that are organic. Many common plant foods may make the flowers pretty, but can actually poison birds, small animals, and people!

17◎ **Speak out against pollution.** Believe it or not, even though a company is taking the risk of causing terrible illness and disease by polluting the environment, and can pay millions of dollars in fines if they are caught, some still try to get away with doing it. Is a manufacturing company near you dumping hazardous chemicals into the ground? Is waste water being piped into streams and rivers? Don't be afraid to write to your local newspaper to protest. Don't forget, people pollute, too. If someone is dumping trash illegally or burning leaves and branches when they aren't supposed to do it, remind them politely that we share this planet and they don't have the right to foul it up for you.

171 **Tell your parents about compact fluorescents.** Your family can replace almost every one of the common light bulbs in your home with a new type called compact fluorescents. They cost much more, but last a lot longer and save tons of electricity. In the long run, they are far cheaper to own and use than standard bulbs. That should sound good to your parents. Saving the earth's resources should sound good to everybody.

172 **Be a water miser.** You can waste two gallons of water by letting the tap run when you brush your teeth! So take short showers, don't use the toilet as a waste basket, and turn off the tap while you're washing the dishes or brushing your teeth. And check for leaks.

173 **Recycle those disposable batteries!** Batteries that power games and other electronic devices like calculators and watches often have dangerous elements in them that can get into our food and water when we throw them away. Pressure your recycling center to take them if they don't already. Then, put a bucket in the lunchroom at school for collection. Another tip—buy and use rechargeable batteries whenever possible. You can charge them and charge them, hundreds of times. They save money and keep poisons out of the earth.

174 **Give your parents booklets about energy efficiency.** Most power utilities make available information about buying and using the most energy-efficient appliances and plugging leaks that waste heat and air conditioning.

175 **C**ollect used telephone books. Kids in Lakewood, Ohio, collect them in a school parking lot. The old phone books then get shredded and used as bedding for animals in the Cleveland Metroparks Zoo.

176 **S**tart a compost pile. Any uncooked vegetable matter—the parts you don't eat from celery, potato peels, carrot shavings, orange skins, and other stuff—can be turned back into rich food for the garden if you compost it with grass clippings from your yard. Composting means letting it naturally rot until it looks almost like soil. Catalogs and home centers sell special bins for composting, but a remote corner of your yard works fine, and if you compost properly there is no bad smell. Some towns even have a common compost heap for residents to use, because it means less garbage to haul and bury.

177 **W**rite about your environmental concerns to pen pals in other countries. One of the projects of Children's Alliance for Protection of the Environment is its international pen pals program, which hooks you up with kids around the world to talk about your environmental activities and ideas. Children's Alliance for Protection of the Environment, P.O. Box 307, Austin, TX 78767.

178 Make a segment for the kids' earth flag.
Kids for a Clean Environment is creating a flag made up of squares showing the way kids see the world. Write them at P.O. Box 158254, Nashville, TN 37215.

179 Rebuild the dunes. Terrible storms in recent years have made a mess of the natural barriers along ocean waters. Your local environmental group needs help restoring them to their proper state.

180 Dig for history in the dirt. Even if you are too young to take part in the scientific work at local archaeological explorations, you will learn a tremendous amount and make a big contribution by assisting researchers—keeping track of supplies, bringing refreshments, etc.

181 Keep plastic out of the sea. Plastic bags and balloons look like jellyfish to some sea animals. They eat the plastic and it makes them die. Make sure you clean up after yourself after a day at the beach.

182 Buy products from environmentalists. An actor who sells popcorn and salad dressing, two fuzzy guys from Vermont who make ice cream, they turn profits into good deeds by giving to environmental and other causes every time you buy their products.

183 Take a volunteer vacation. Instead of just seeing the sites at a national park, you can help improve them for everybody. Instead of eating in junky restaurants, maybe you can help harvest a field of vegetables so hungry folks can have a meal, too. Talk to your family members about turning your week off into a week that really matters. Look for a book called *Eco-Vacations: Enjoy Yourself and the Earth,* by Evelyn Kay, Blue Penguin Publications.

184 Learn about solar power. The sun is a furnace, a light source, and power plant all in one! Find out how, with just the sun's rays, you can heat your water, cook a hamburger, power a video game and TV, recharge your batteries, and keep a soft drink cold.

And Here Are Some More:

185 Use recycled paper and water-based paints and markers for art projects.

186 Buy soft drinks in glass bottles or aluminum cans; they can be recycled more easily and completely than plastic.

187 **J**oin a national environmental organization. Look for groups with a particular em-
phasis on projects and causes kids can support.

188 **B**e a trailblazer. Your parks commission
needs help every year cleaning up the trails
through nature preserves and parks.

189 **B**uy a live Christmas tree. Plant it after
the holiday.

190 **B**ring a backpack when you shop, and
refuse those little plastic bags.

191 **B**e an acid rain detective. Monitor the
amount of acid in rain water where you live
for the National Audubon Society, 700 Broadway,
New York, NY 10003-9562.

192 **K**eep a litter bag in the car.

193 **R**efuse plastic forks and spoons with
take-out food you bring home.

194 **U**se a lunch box instead of throw-away
bags.

195 Try a rag or cloth by the sink instead of wasteful paper towels.

196 Burn energy on your bike instead of burning gas in the car.

197 Take charge of recycling at school.

198 Post Save Water signs in your apartment building or in your town during draught emergencies.

199 Work at your Audubon Society book-store.

With Your Friends, Club or Group

200 Celebrate Earth Day. April 22 is the day celebrated around the world to raise everybody's awareness of the need to conserve energy, look for new ways to power cars and other vehicles that don't waste resources and pollute the air, and keep the environment safe for plants and animals. Each year, people get together to clean parks and replant gardens, talk about their efforts to stop pollution, and enjoy a beautiful spring day. Join the festivities where you live, or plan your own observance. For information: Earth Day USA, 20 Grove Street, Box 470, Peterborough, NH 03458.

201 Save the rainforest. Tropical forests, that is, forests close to the earth's equator, are very old and hold a lot of secrets scientists want to explore. There's no question the giant trees in the rainforest create a lot of oxygen for us to breathe. Beyond that, there is great hope the leaves and roots of plants that grow there (and nowhere else on earth!) might be useful for curing many diseases, including cancer. Yet, every year many trees are cut down for their lumber—an area the size of West Virginia is cleared each year, and often not replanted properly. Kids have led the effort to save the rainforest. You can actually buy a piece of it, to protect it forever. Write to The Children's Rainforest, P.O. Box 936, Lewiston, ME 04240; or call (207) 784-1069.

202 Play an environmental game. Members of Animal Tracks, an environmental education program in Arkansas elementary schools, play a new form of tag—you can be tagged "it" when you can't call out the name of a recycled product!

203 Create a forest. Planting a tree or two is a great idea, but if your whole class plants tree seedlings on barren ground, you can have a forest by the time you are adults!

204 Adopt a creek. The Community Creek Watch project in Santa Clara County, California, is devoted to studying the condition of creeks throughout its area because of their importance to wildlife. They keep track of the animals and plant life, the condition of the water, and any changes that might show a dangerous condition for the animals and birds that use creeks for water, nesting, shelter, and food sources. They train people from age eight to eighty the science they need to know and how to collect information. Since perhaps half of all birds and mammals use creeks and streams, and stream and creek beds might be the last place you can find some native plants and grasses, knowing how well those habitats are surviving is important to all of us. Write Community Creek Watch at Coyote Creek Riparian Station, P.O. Box 1027, Alviso, CA 95002.

205 Learn to spot excessive packaging. In class, compare similar products you might buy and see which of them use less paper, cardboard, and plastic just to package the thing.

206 Keep native plants alive. The Ballona Wetlands in Los Angeles is an area of natural dunes and marsh that is home to many varieties of wild animals and plants. But the wetlands are threatened by other plants that have invaded the territory and are choking the life out of the environment. Volunteers—kids included—go out with bags, tools, and gloves to clear unwelcome vegetation. If you live in an area with a similar problem, talk to your local environmental group about getting involved. And remember—wear old shoes and take along a sun screen; it's hot and mucky out there!

207 Test your water. You drink the water at school all day long, but is it safe? Sometimes harmful chemicals or waste products turn up in drinking water when the water source is too close to factories or other businesses. Make sure your water is tested regularly if you suspect any dangers.

208 Ask your town officials to "keep it green." Attend meetings where they are planning to build projects that wipe out woods or might pollute the water, and let them know they are spoiling your future.

209 If you send cookies to relatives or friends, instead of wasting paper or Styrofoam to keep those cookies from crumbling, pack them in somethng edible—popcorn!

210 Make conservation posters. Alert your friends and classmates to the dangers of environmental pollution and display your work on the classroom walls.

2ll **M**ark storm drains. From *Nick News:* Kids from Martins, California, found out people were using storm drains—those iron grates along the streets and roads that are meant to carry rain water away from roads—to dump paint and other harmful household chemicals. "When we dump pollutants it gets into the creek and all the pesticides and stuff kill the animals in there," says one kid. Now, the kids put signs on the sidewalk: No Dumping. Drains into the Creek! so people know anything they toss down the hole will foul the water.

2l2 **S**ponsor an environmental slogan contest. Can you come up with a phrase that sums up why it's important to keep the planet safe? Compete against your friends to see whose is best.

2l3 **B**ang on doors. Working with an established group (and an adult to take you around), you can spread the word for an environmental cause by going door to door and telling people about your crusade. Whether it's to get donations or ask them to write to their state assemblypersons, most people have a harder time slamming the door in the face of a kid than they would in the face of an adult!

214 Recycle discarded refrigerator boxes into toy cars, boats, and houses for small children.

215 Ask if your school uses recycled paper.

CLEAN

DOING OUR PART FOR CREATURES WHO NEED HELP.

Alissa Jones couldn't believe the news. The whole idea sounded like a dream come true.

Her mother had just found out about a new place called the Horse Rescue Center in Underwood, Minnesota, hours and hours from Minneapolis, where Alissa lives. The center is a special farm for horses that are sick, abandoned by their owners, or mistreated, her mother told her. Started by a family called the Seviours, the farm keeps the horses until they are well, then they go to good families that will take care of them properly.

Eight-year-old Alissa loves horses, so she was happy for them. But the next part made her freak out. The Joneses own a little cabin not far from the Horse Rescue Center, and according to the news story Alissa's mother read, the center depends on volunteers

Alissa's age who can come to the center and stay for free as long as they work hard.

Finally, a chance.

Could this really be happening? Could Alissa, who has loved horses since she was about three, really get a chance to touch them, feed them, and take care of them?

"It really excited me too much," says Alissa. "I sat right down and wrote a letter telling them I wanted to be a volunteer. I got back a letter saying the next time we were in Underwood I should come to visit."

The trip from Minneapolis to Underwood takes about three and a half hours, but at their first opportunity, the Joneses planned a weekend at the cabin that would include a visit to the Horse Rescue Center.

When they got there, they found out the center is really bare bones: one barn plus one they are fixing up, a pasture with fencing that seems always to need mending, no luxurious accommodations for the visitors and volunteers, who stay mostly in sleeping bags on the floor. The center gets most of what it needs from donations, and among the things it needs most is help from people who care.

Future owners are carefully chosen.

Since many of the horses at the center are malnourished and underweight when they first arrive, the center is very careful about who gets to adopt the animals when they are well. Potential owners are screened and interviewed the same way they would be if they were adopting a baby! Even the volunteers who work at the center are carefully considered. No one who has ever abused an animal or another person is allowed near the horses.

"When we got there, I met Karen Seviour outside and she took me around and told me the names of all the horses," Alissa remembers. "Then we went inside to talk.

"Karen told me all of the things I would be doing there. Things like putting medicine on the horses, making fences, feeding the horses, cleaning the stalls—actually, I haven't done that part yet."

A chance to learn and a chance to help.

Before working at the center, Alissa's only experiences with horses were the one time she rode a pony at a birthday party and the one time she got to ride a horse on a farm near the Jones's cabin. Suddenly, she was brushing them, learning how to put on and take off a saddle, trimming their hooves, and learning to mount and dismount, balance, and trot.

Just being around them was thrilling for her, but knowing she was doing something to help horses made it even more special. "Some of them were sick and needed medicine, or were scared of people," she says. "Now, they are becoming my friends. They smell my hand, and they know me."

In mid July, Alissa finally got to spend a whole week at the center with five to ten kids her age. They woke up early, ate donated food, and worked hard. But it was worth it.

"It makes me feel good to know I'm helping," she says.

Alissa was given professional training before she worked with the animals at the Horse Rescue Center, and in a lot of cases kids who want to care for animals should get proper instruction first. That is especially true when you're dealing with animals that may be sick or injured.

FIX A PROBLEM:

To help save horses that might die or be slaughtered without proper care and foster homes, contact the Horse Rescue Center, c/o Seviour, RR1 Box 13A, Underwood, MN 56586. Their phone number is (218) 826-6899.

Animals in the wild.

Lots of kids worry about injured animals that live in the woods, fields, and trees, but trying to rescue wildlife by themselves isn't always a great idea for kids. "They aren't prepared for the constant care an injured animal needs. You might have to feed it in the middle of the night," says Nancy Rubin of Wildlife Rescue in Palo Alto, California.

One thirteen-year old found out just how difficult it is when a young grackle fell from its tree in her yard.

"I called a vet and asked her what to do," says Jamie Kouns, Cocoa Beach, Florida, who named the bird Nite Shaide. "I ended up feeding that baby every thirty minutes while I was home. Finally, I let him loose in our backyard."

Over-rescuing animals that aren't really injured is another danger. It's actually quite common for birds to spend some time on the ground when they are still learning to fly. That's why Wildlife Rescue officials recommend kids raise money to donate for rescues rather than attemping them. But they are happy to speak to school groups about wild animals, and will sometimes let them watch the spectacular moment when a healthy animal is released back into the wild.

Special bond.

Kids who care about animals often end up with a lifetime concern for helping other species. "I have a strange interest in birds and really enjoy them," says Jamie. "Hopefully one day I'll get to work with real birds and help save one on my own."

If you have an animal shelter or veterinary hospital near your home, or even a kennel where dogs need grooming or exercise, then those could be good places to look for animals that need care. But don't forget the birds right near your home, either. Some fresh water in a bird bath and bird feeders full of seeds are always important sources of water and food, and they are most important during the winter when birds that don't fly south have trouble finding food to eat.

To help animals that need you, consider this list of ideas:

On Your Own or With Your Family

216 Visit **a horse rescue center.** While the Horse Rescue Center in Underwood, Minnesota, may be the only one that allows young volunteers like Alissa Jones, you can visit and learn about the important work they do at other centers in Minnesota, as well as in Wisconsin, Colorado, California, and other states.

217 Care **for animals at the children's zoo.** Petting zoos, where kids can get really close to farm creatures, snakes, and birds, help small children learn respect for other animals. You can become an expert on where animals live, what they eat, and who their enemies are, and help small children satisfy their natural curiosity.

218 Participate **in a whale watch.** A great family vacation idea—you're on board an ocean vessel with scientists trying to keep track of the world's whale population, which is in danger from over-hunting and other threats. Search parties go looking in spots where whales should be, count the number they see, and report back. A few organizations permit kids to come along with their families. Write: American Cetacean Society, P.O. Box 2639, San Pedro, CA 90731; Oceanic Society Expeditions, Fort Mason Center, Building E, San Francisco, CA 94123; Eye of the Whale, P.O. Box 1269, Kapa'au, HI 96755.

219 Adopt an animal. Your local animal shelter has dozens of really cute dogs and cats that are safe, healthy, and ready for adoption. Everybody knows that mutts make the best pets!

220 Build a bird feeder. Coat a pine cone with peanut butter and roll it in seeds. Or cut the bottom off a two-liter soft-drink bottle, use a couple of aluminim pie plates as the top and bottom, fill with seeds, and stick a stretched-out coat hanger through the whole thing so you can hang it from a tree limb. Those are just two easy bird feeders you can make from items around the house. You can make a bird bath, too, out of a ceramic dish suspended from a tree.

221 Participate in the Backyard Habitat Program. The National Wildlife Federation encourages everyone to create animal habitats, or living places, where we work, live, go to school, and play. They provide instructional pamphlets for members about how to help animals by planting trees, shrubs, and flowers that provide nourishment, water, places to hide, and places to raise their young. National Wildlife Federation, Backyard Habitat Program, 1412 16th Street NW, Washington, DC 20036.

222 Cut up soft-drink six-pack rings. Those plastic gizmos that hold soft drink cans together can get caught around a bird's beak or a baby seal's neck. The animals then suffocate or starve. Just by snipping each ring with scissors before discarding it, you can save an animal's life.

And Here Are Some More:

223 Join Zero Population Growth. Learn the environmental dangers of overpopulation and help spread the word. Call (202) 332-2200.

224 Volunteer at a stable in return for riding lessons.

225 Assist at an animal hospital.

226 Brush, walk, and exercise animals at the animal shelter.

227 Take care of the critters at your school.

228 Work at the pet store.

229 Be a grounds keeper at the zoo.

230 Call the ASPCA or dog catcher to rescue stray dogs.

231 Attend a wildlife summer camp.

232 Ask your parents to use humane mouse traps that don't kill animals.

233 Don't disturb birds' nests you find in trees, fields, and barns.

234 Make sure your pets have proper shots.

235 Remember to play with your pets.

With Your Friends, Club or Group

236 Raise money for endangered species.

The more land we pave for parking lots, or forests we clear for wood products and house construction, the more we chip away at the land animals have to live their natural lives. In some countries, animals such as tigers are killed for sport, even though their numbers are dwindling. And elephants, those majestic giants, are often senselessly hacked to death just for their ivory tusks. Here is just a short list of animals in danger: wolves, turtles, mustangs, whales, manatees, and tigers. Write to Defenders of Wildlife, 1101 14th Street NW, Suite 1400, Washington, DC 20035, or call them at (202) 682-9400.

237 Schedule a presentation by a wildlife rescue expert. It takes experience to know how to work in the wild and nurse animals back to health. In some instances, Wildlife Rescue in Palo Alto, California, will let you watch the release of an animal once it's healthy. In other parts of the country, find wildlife rescue groups through The International Wildlife Rehabilitation Council, 4437 Central Place, Suite B4, Suisun, CA 94585.

238 Keep wild animals on their land. From *Nick News:* On a section of the Ozark National Scenic Riverways in Missouri, about twenty wild horses roam free. The Park Service wanted to remove the horses to keep them off protected land, but the Missouri Wild Horse League, a group of adults and kids determined to save them, fought back. Protestors included Ginger Krisko, thirteen, who sees the horses when she goes riding and thinks they are a beautiful and special thing. The protest worked, for now: the Park Service has agreed to temporarily suspend any action until they reach a compromise with the Missouri Wild Horse League.

23 ♀ Find out if your school cafeteria is serving dolphin-safe tuna. Not so long ago, tuna fishermen around the world used nets that would also trap dolphins by accident. These beautiful, intelligent sea mammals were being killed for no reason. After a lot of pressure from people, including kids, to switch to a different kind of net, the largest companies switched to dolphin-safe techniques. Check with your school cafeteria to make sure the tuna they buy is from a company that uses humane methods to catch its fish.

24 ◎ Start an animal help club. Does it bother you that animals raised for their meat, milk, and eggs are often farmed as though they were in a factory, crowded into little pens or cages with little opportunity to see the sun or walk freely? Do you think it's fair the way animals are used to test products for people, even before the products are known to be safe? Why do some people say it's important to neuter your household pets, like dogs and cats? Get professionals who know about these practices to speak to your group, then make noise about the practices you think are wrong.

And Here Are Some More:

241 Volunteer at the aquarium. You may not get to feed and care for the animals right from the start, but doing office chores and helping visitors will teach you a lot about the exhibits and the work that goes into helping wildlife.

242 Create an extinct animal gallery. Learn about animals that no longer exist in the world, and draw their pictures for a display. Help people learn the importance of rescuing animals that may not survive modern times.

243 Become a human zoo. Teach young kids about animals from around the world by dressing up in costumes and putting on a play about them.

244 Share farm animals with city kids. One 4-H project gives kids an opportunity to learn about life on the farm and a greater appreciation for the animals there by letting them visit and help feed the livestock.

245 Give farm tours. "The 4-H kids staff these. Each kid presents the animal he or she knows most about to the tourist as a ten to fifteen minute talk about the breed's history and basic care of the animal." Corinna Schembari, 4-H member, Hanover, Massachusetts.

246 Join a critter count. Ever wonder how an island night lizard or a black oyster-catcher winds up on the endangered species list? Somebody goes out and counts them first. The volunteer Student Conservation Association sends older kids out for the summer to work with biologists and researchers six days a week counting populations of birds and other wildlife on government land all around the country. The Student Conservation Association, (603) 543-1700.

247 Ask at the zoo if you can adopt one of the animals. Contributions go toward its care and feeding.

248 March in an all-species parade. Show off your pets and farm livestock in the Memorial Day or other parade to take pride in our interdependence.

249 Appear on a public access TV show to talk about pet care.

STAYiNG HeALTHY, HeLPiNG THe SiCK

HOW KIDS CAN TAKE AN ACTIVE PART IN
CARING AND CURING.

Pling!! Whirr!! "Welcome! You have mail!"

The computer monitor blinks alive with a message. It's from ReesesBear, the code name of a kid who keeps in touch with friends on the computer service, America Online. According to the message, Reeses-Bear has a special project: she wants to help kids who are stuck in hospitals.

"I am writing a newsletter," say the words appearing across the screen. "I thought it would be a good idea. The newsletter will have four to six pages, and we will mail it to as many hospitals as we can find listed with pediatric wards," meaning hospitals that do special medicine just for sick children.

"The newsletter will have stories, jokes/riddles, community news, class projects, poems, kids who care, some games to do, etc. It even has a pull out section so kids can have a pen pal and won't be so lonely.''

The newsletter, called the *Bearable Times,* will be written by ReesesBear and her classmates, with contributions from other America Online subscribers.

A mystery.

But who is this mysterious ReesesBear, whose messages appear in the night? Where did she get her wild, totally cool name? And most important of all, why does she care so much about kids in the hospital?

The answer to the last question is the easiest to answer: she cares about kids in the hospital because she was one herself.

"I am Alexis," writes Alexis Brown, finally revealing her real name. "I am 10 and in the fifth grade at Harwich Middle School (East Harwich, Massachusetts). I was born with Cerebral Palsy."

But the cerebral palsy, as challenging as it is for her, isn't what put her in the hospital last year. During the winter, Alexis felt as if she had the flu, but she couldn't get better. The doctors finally found out she had lupus, another disease that required a long hospital stay and lots of treatment. Even today, she is still trying to get well.

Just lying around.

"I was in the hospital for almost six weeks," she remembers. "It was not fun. I missed my family. My mom stayed with me the whole time. And I only saw my sister Victoria (HipHopTori, to America Online friends) and my brother Isaiah (BurgerKid) twice, and my dad and relatives came to visit me, too.''

Sure, she got mail, and lots of visitors, but one thing made enjoying the attention hard for her. ''I noticed that kids did not get any mail when I was sick in bed,'' she says. ''I got mail, but I felt bad for the other kids who were really sick like me.''

Right now, Alexis's family is paying the cost of producing the newsletter, but they hope to get donations. Alexis has a logo, designed by someone who writes and illustrates children's books, and one idea to get more money for the newsletter is to print and sell T-shirts with the logo. Alexis hopes the *Bearable Times* can become a non-profit corporation and expand its interests to include family members of kids who are sick, ''Especially brothers and sisters, because sometimes it's hard for them, and scary, too!''

WHAT TO Do:

To send jokes, stories, news, or happy messages to kids in the hospital through the *Bearable Times*, send to ReesesBear on America Online. Or write to the *Bearable Times*, P.O. Box 533, East Harwich, MA 02645. Or phone (508) 432-4975.

Alexis is also writing a story about her time in the hospital, and hopes other kids with similar experiences will be contributors to the *Bearable Times*. ''Writing about your feelings can make you feel better,'' she says. "I hope the newsletter will make them happy and let them know people care about them. Plus they will make some special friendships if they decide to fill out the pen pal sheet. I think it will be awesome!"

So that leaves only one mystery about ReesesBear to solve: "I love bears, and eating Reeses!" she says.

There's a lot you can do first to promote good health in your community, like spreading the word about the dangers of smoking, or getting your school to sponsor a health fair. For people who are already sick, you can help them with simple chores, or jus† be there to let them know somebody cares. Hospitals and other care centers often depend on volunteers—there's always way too much to do!

Check out this check list for an activity you may want to try.

On Your Own Or With Your Family

250 ◎ Contribute to the *Bearable Times*. See address above.

251 Be a hospital volunteer. As a front desk attendant, you'll answer phones, make deliveries, discharge patients. If you can cheer them up, even for a minute or two, you'll be doing something important for the patients and something rewarding for you.

252 "**I volunteered at the Red Cross at one of their fundraisers.** They had a field day at a local park. I was the Red Cross mascot, DAT Bear (Disaster and Training). I sat in this hot, sweaty costume for about four or five hours, and helped raise a few thousand dollars for the organization." Charlie Pabst, fourteen, Glendale, Arizona.

253 Create a living memory. The Names Project in San Francisco maintains a quilt made of panels memorializing people who have died of AIDS, and people of all ages from around the world take part in making it and repairing panels. (415) 882-5500.

254 Spread the word about AIDS. Project AHEAD in San Francisco sends young people with the virus that causes AIDS to speak to other kids about the disease, and publishes a newsletter by the kids themselves. (415) 487-5777.

255 Make tray favors for little kids. Small gifts that show up on trays are a nice surprise at meal time.

256 Do a home safety audit. Make sure dangerous chemicals and household cleaners aren't where little kids can get to them, that poisons are properly labeled, loose wiring is repaired, etc.

257 Participate in mock disaster training. Medical emergency response teams need make-believe victims so they can practice what to do if there is a fire, earthquake, or tornado. Hey, just think—you can help by lying on the ground moaning with a lot of fake blood on you! Talk to your school nurse or rescue squad.

258 Become part of a HamNet. Are you one of the thousands of ham radio fans across the country? Often, they are the first people to get the word out when there's been a natural disaster, such as a flood or a storm. You can save sick or injured people by helping rescue workers pinpoint the spot where assistance is needed.

259 Join the American Red Cross Youth Volunteer Service Program. You can be effective in a number of areas, such as working at a veterans' hospital, speaking to community groups, getting disaster preparedness training, and more.

And Here Are
Some More:

260 Tell your parents to stop smoking.

261 Take a drug-free pledge with every member of your family.

262 Call a sick friend.

263 Join an AIDS walk to raise money.

264 Be a bike messenger for an ill neighbor.

265 Bring gifts to sick kids.

266 Send cards to a hospital pen pal.

267 Give old eyeglasses you can't use to a pharmacy that collects them for people who can't afford new ones.

268 Give used crutches to a health clinic.

269 Donate toys to a pediatric ward.

270 Tape a story and give it to a children's hospital.

With Your Friends, Club, or Group

271 **Learn lifesaving skills.** You never know when an emergency is going to strike, so it's good to know the rules about calling an ambulance, how to help someone who has been hurt, and what you should do if someone has stopped breathing or their heart isn't beating. The local chapter of The American Red Cross can send someone to your school or club to train you, or you can take classes at the Red Cross headquarters. There are many stories about kids as young as two years old who have saved a life because they knew what to do!

272 **Organize a drug summit in your school,** where representatives from every grade can talk about the dangers of illegal drugs with health officials and police from your town.

273 **Help babies with AIDS.** Among the projects of Kids Connection, Inc. in Tustin, California, is the organization's drive to collect diapers, baby food, and clothing for families of kids with AIDS. At holiday time, the group adds festive foods and toys for the sick kids and their brothers and sisters.

274 **Join D.A.R.E.** Drug Awareness Resistance Education groups are everywhere, and help kids spread the word to other kids to live clean.

275 Decorate a Happy Hat for Kids. The medicines they give to people being treated for cancer or AIDS can make them lose their hair. Happy Hats for Kids tries to make the experience a little less unhappy for kids by creating fun hats with bows, flowers, sports designs, shiny stuff, and anything else you can do. Kids as young as seven do the designing with their Brownie and Cub Scout troops, or on their own, and more than 8,000 hats have been decorated and given away so far. To get information on how you can help, call founder Sheri Galper at (818) 713-1775.

276 Assist the Red Cross at Bloodmobiles. You're probably too young to roll up your sleeve and let them squeeze out a pint of the red stuff, but you can help distribute forms and pass out cookies and drinks to people who need a little energy boost after they donate blood.

277 Work to establish smoking bans. What? They haven't passed a law yet where you live making it illegal to smoke in public places? Well, what are you going to do about it? Wait until you're choking to death? Circulate a petition, send it to your state legislators, follow up with letters to your representatives demanding action! Why not? They're your lungs, right? Start using them to make some noise!

27 8 Read fairy tales to kids. The emergency room can be a pretty scary and confusing place for kids, with nothing but adults running around and no place to play. Make it easier on them by reading familiar fairy tales and stories that will put them at ease. Talk to your hospital volunteer administrator, or your school nurse.

27 9 Give a party for health care workers. Show your appreciation for doctors or rescue squad members in your community by throwing them a blast.

28 0 Bring joy to the ward. Take your chorus to hospitals at Christmas time, and carol from room to room.

28 1 Perform gymnastics at the hospital. Patients receiving long-term care need entertainment to pass the time. See if your hospital has an auditorium large enough for presentations.

282 Decorate the hospital for the holidays.
When you are in a mood to celebrate, don't forget the people who need extra cheer.

And Here Are
Some More:

283 Be a clown. Dress up silly, paint your faces, make some kids smile in the hospital.

284 Write and perform a play about being in the hospital. Make it easier on little kids about to go through an operation.

285 Help in the hospital gift shop. Assist by putting prices on things, counting what's available to sell, and selling items to customers.

286 Sponsor a health fair. Learn from professionals what to eat, how to exercise, what to do in an emergency.

HOW KIDS CAN HELP OLDER AMERICANS LIVE A BETTER LIFE.

Smear Vaseline on the inside of a pair of sunglasses and try to read a page from your favorite book. Tie bean bags to your shoes and walk across the room. Have a friend tape or tie your thumbs to your fingers on each hand and try to tie your shoes.

Difficult? Frustrating? Imagine living every day with those kinds of challenges, and you'll understand a little more what it's like to grow older and have your body age and change.

Kids around the country who volunteer to help other citizens through the National Center for Service Learning in Early Adolescence first try exercises like these. They perform the exercises in pairs of one "senior" and one "non-senior"; that's to learn not only what it feels like to need assistance, but also to get a sense of when, as a volunteer, you should help, and when you should let the older person feel independent.

Older people like what you like.

When you get older, sometimes you have to slow down a bit. Maybe your fingers hurt, or you don't see as well as you used to see. But even people in wheelchairs like to go to dances to hear the music and enjoy the company. People with trouble reading still like books and stories, they just need someone else to read to them. In fact, people like the same things in their old age that they liked when they were kids: parties, music, treats, crafts, and most of all, friends.

In even the smallest communities, senior centers are the places where older citizens gather for companionship and activities. The centers often have such a big schedule of activities planned for their members that finding a way to participate is easy.

You may also want to *be* the activity for a day. Check the suggestion list for ideas about taking your singing group or class play to the local senior center for a day.

Other ways to help.

For older people who need more help to get along, residential care homes exist where they can go to live and be sure of having professionals take care of their daily needs. Age restrictions may make it a little more difficult for you to be involved with the seniors on a personal basis, but many of these homes have recre-

○ ○

ation rooms where you may be welcome to play the piano for the residents, call bingo numbers, or join them in exercise classes.

Right on your street, you may have older neighbors who are home-bound, and the list of ways you and your family can be helpful to them is endless. Even active seniors will appreciate your extra hands taking care of chores and running errands for them.

PAY A **Visit**:

To be a friend to an older person, see if there's a Department on Aging office in your town, or contact the Youth Service America (YSA) office for suggestions. The National Center for Service Learning in Early Adolescence, 25 West 43rd Street, Suite 612, New York, NY 10036, can also help you find any kind of volunteer activity you might like, including working with older people. Talk to your guidance counselor about it. Also, ask your clergyperson about volunteer opportunities with elderly citizens. Watch your local newspaper or TV news for announcements of events aimed at helping seniors.

An important thing to remember is, when you start helping seniors, you are bound to get hooked! You might be scared at first, or think you'll be bored hanging around people who are seventy or eighty years old. But many kids who have tried different ways of volunteering say helping older people can be the most fun. They appreciate the simplest gestures of kindness and friendship, and really care about you, too. They'll want to hear about your family, your friends, and the things that interest you.

Try one of these activities.

On Your Own or With Your Family

287 **Deliver meals on wheels.** Your folks will need to supply the wheels, but taking prepared dinners to older people who are stuck at home, unable to shop or cook, is a great volunteer project. And the organization Meals on Wheels that supplies and cooks the meals makes it a snap. They assign you a route and hand you the dinners. All you need to add is the smile when you ring the doorbell.

288 **Take an older person shopping.** In most communities, driving is a real necessity. Older people can end up staying home when they would rather be out because they can no longer drive. Next time you and the family are going mall trawling, why not ask an elderly neighbor along for the ride?

289 **Help an older person decorate for holidays.** Christmas and other holidays are special times of the year to share. But older people may have trouble lifting heavy boxes full of decorations from the attic, or hanging pretty things from high places. Your strong back and creativity can help them have a happy holiday.

290 Cut and rake lawns. Some kids do this work to make some extra cash, but you can cash in on an older person's gratitude by doing yard work as a favor.

291 Devote an afternoon to crafts. Try this: you sign your name, then your senior friend signs his or her name. Then, each of you tries to draw an animal out of the other person's signature. Or, color a flag from the country where your senior friend's family originated. Before you know it, you'll be swapping stories about your families, or talking about famous people who share your names. You can probably come up with a hundred different arts and crafts projects to enjoy together.

292 Be an older person's eyes. Read to someone who can no longer read alone. Books, magazine articles, or today's paper all interest an older person who wants to stay in touch with what's happening in the world. Don't be surprised if your friend asks your opinion of what you're reading. Older people really care what kids think!

293 Read a book on tape. If you can't get to a senior center to visit in person, you can still make a contribution by reading a popular book into a tape recorder.

294 Visit. One of the best gifts you can give to someone who is lonely is your company. You don't need a special talent, and you don't have to wait for a special holiday. All you need is the ability to love someone who is waiting to love you back.

295 Be a greenhouse volunteer. If you love tending plants, assist at residence homes where they have greenhouses.

296 Sew walker bags for the elderly. Older people who rely on walkers to get around need a place to stash their purchases and belongings. If you sew, you can make their errands easier to perform with a cloth bag that attaches to the walker they use.

297 Help an older person around the house. Change a light bulb, hang a picture, climb on a step stool to fetch something out of reach.

And Here Are Some More:

298 Help an older person whose hand isn't steady write letters.

299 Take music cassettes to play for an older friend.

300 Teach an older shut-in some fun card games.

301 Wash a senior's car.

302 Help an older person do garden work.

303 If a blizzard or hurricane is on the way, make sure a senior on your block has essential water, canned goods, etc.

304 Help an elderly person care for pets.

305 Play piano for residents in a retirement home.

306 Pick up the morning newspaper for a senior neighbor.

307 Be a bike messenger. Pick up prescriptions and other necessities for someone who is stuck at home.

308 Take a plant to friend at a senior residence.

309 Send your senior friend a valentine.

310 Press a pretty flower flat and make a wall decoration.

311 Take out and return library books for an older person.

312 Call bingo at the senior drop-in center.

313 Take a walk with a senior neighbor.

With Your Friends, Club, or Group

314 Throw a "senior" prom. Plan a real blast at your local senior center or residence home. Help the staff plan the refreshments and the entertainment (choose music your senior friends will like). Make tissue paper flowers for all the men and women to wear, and decorate the recreation room with lots of colored streamers. Then, dress up and enjoy the evening with your guests.

315 Perform your step squad routine. Do you and your friends get together after school to rehearse your steps? Why not make someone else's afternoon by going to the senior center to show off your talent? And while we're on the subject . . .

316 Give a command performance of your school talent show. Talk to your teacher or drama coach about organizing a private performance of your talent show or class play for culture-loving seniors who can travel to your school auditorium. Or, take the show on the road! Try to organize an after-school showcase at the residence home recreation room.

317 Plan a make-over day. Many people in residence homes have difficulty doing even the simplest tasks, but everyone likes to look nice.

You can help by touching up the women's makeup, or combing the men's hair.

318 Assist at Senior Day at the mall. A 4-H club in California takes care of a whole range of duties when the local Target store had Senior Day at Christmas time. The kids help older shoppers by pushing their wheelchairs, shopping with them, serving refreshments, and wrapping packages.

319 Create an oral history. Interview seniors about their lives and experiences on audio tape, and document the world that used to be.

320 Be a cheerleader at a walk-a-thon. Thousands of walkers each year participate in the Golden Gait Walk-a-thon in San Francisco to benefit the group Self Help for the Elderly. Walkers who sign up get friends and family to pledge money to the charity if the walker completes the course. Similar events take place all across the country, and walkers come in all sizes and ages. But if you'd like to help in another way, your scout troop can be the cheerleading squad at the finish line, or route markers along the way.

321 Serve meals at a residence home. Meal time is always hectic, and extra help is often appreciated. By scheduling a regular day for your club to volunteer serving, you can help the home save money for other residents' needs.

322 **D**ecorate the dining hall for Thanksgiving. Thanksgiving's a big day for senior centers, since many seniors are alone with no one close to them to share their holiday meal. Hundreds of volunteers set thousands of place settings in every city, and you can make the day even more festive by decorating the walls and tables with harvest themes and pictures of turkeys, pilgrims, and native Americans.

323 **"O**ne of our projects is to take animals to nursing homes and our local V.A. hospital. We have taken dogs, baby pygmy goats, baby dairy goats, sheep, rabbits, cavies [guinea pigs to the uninitiated], and assorted pocket pets." Corinna Schembari, 4-H member, Hanover, Massachusetts.

And Here Are Some More:

324 **Start a Christmas card club.** Get the names of senior home residents and make sure they are remembered at holiday time.

325 **Lead an exercise class.**

326 **Plan a picnic for senior citizens.**

VISIT

DOING OUR PART FOR FRIENDS
IN OTHER LANDS.

You may be looking at a map at school one day and suddenly find yourself thinking, I wonder what the people there are like? Perhaps a new neighbor with an unfamiliar accent moves next door to your family. You wonder, What is it like in their home country?

Kids are naturally curious about people in other countries, and are especially interested in kids their age. They write to pen pals, learn dances and songs from other nations, and read stories about what life is like where the weather, the food, and the culture are very different from theirs.

One of the reasons kids care so much about kids growing up in other places is, unless you are the descendant of a native American, your family came from somewhere else. Your parents or your parents' parents or someone related to you a hundred years ago came to this country looking for a better life. We look at how we live, and look at how people live in other lands, and wonder how much we've changed!

When disaster strikes.

Sometimes, a shocking story wakes us up to the poor conditions people face in other countries. You may read about a war where innocent people die or a terrible flood or earthquake that killed thousands. A country whose name is new to you may be suffering a shortage of water and food that is slowly starving people every day. Then, we stop being curious and start wanting to help.

But what can you do for people thousands and thousands of miles away?

Most of the time, the only way to help is to send money. Many organizations exist in the United States to trade those dollars in for food, medical supplies, and technical help in building roads, clean water facilities, and hospitals. In fact, there are so many charitable groups around that it would be impossible to list them all. (If you decide to raise money for an organization that accepts donations, make sure you look at the chapter on fund raising for some tips and cautions.)

Other groups have as their goal just establishing some bond between people. It may be possible for your class to link up with a class across the globe and learn all about life there. Through your letters and pictures and the art work you draw, you will be sharing your experiences in turn with them.

The goal is peace.

Why is it so important to understand life outside the United States? A lot of people think that the more you know about someone who is different from you, the less likely it is that we will ever go to war with those people or feel hatred toward people who move here from other countries.

Next time at school when you are studying people from another country, try to put yourself in their place. Think about what you'd miss if you lived there. Then, think about the ways their life sounds better than ours. Just because people don't have all the same conveniences we have doesn't mean their lives aren't richer in another way.

Then, let your interest be the fuel that makes you active in helping and sharing. Use one of the ideas in this list as a jumping off point.

On Your Own or With Your Family

327 Scare up donations for UNICEF. Practically every kid knows about trick-or-treating for UNICEF, the United Nations organization that helps hungry kids all around the world. Collection cans are available through your school, or by contacting UNICEF. And the good news is, when you ask for donations instead of candy, most people give you the candy anyway!

328 Adopt a foster brother or sister. You probably see the commercials on television and the ads in magazines and newspapers. Lots of organizations help you pay for the food and school supplies of kids in countries where people are starving and living conditions are very poor. The money you send goes toward the care of one individual child, who will send you letters and pictures from time to time so you can see how your foster sibling is doing.

329 Volunteer for a politcal campaign. Lick envelopes, prepare mailings, learn how the political process works to make change you feel is important.

330 Eat a meatless meal. Animals that turn into hamburger and steak feed a small percentage of the earth's population. But the food we feed to cattle and livestock could feed all the people who starve to death each year.

331 Learn about the world. Encourage people of different racial backgrounds to speak to your class about their culture.

With Your Friends, Club, or Group

332 Give peace a chance. Kids in the Long Island (New York) Student Coalition for Peace and Justice, in Westbury, meet weekly to discuss human rights, civil rights, and other issues that concern them. Their Peace Day, held in May, brought together committed students and speakers. "We're trying to raise the awareness of other students and make them active," said one student organizer.

333 Save someone's eyesight. There's not much you can buy today with four or five pennies, but that's all it takes to keep a kid from going blind. With your pennies, the International Eye

Foundation can help kids in Central America, Africa, and Eastern Europe who are in danger of losing their eyesight. One reason is, they don't get enough vitamins in their foods. The pennies pay for vitamin pills they give to village children. They also teach the parents of those kids which foods to plant that contain the important vitamins. If you sponsor a Penny Drive, here's where to send the dough: 7801 Norfolk Ave., Bethesda, MD 20814.

334 Link arms with kids across the globe.
According to the founder, Perhaps Kids Meeting Kids Can Make a Difference is a group originally formed in 1982 when it arranged the first meeting ever between Soviet and American kids. With the cold war over, the student exchange effort has shifted to getting kids in war-torn countries together with American school kids, and getting kids in warring nations (like those in Israel and Arab countries) together so they can talk. The group is also determined to reduce violence in our own society, and is committed to seeing ratification of the UN Convention on the Rights of a Child. They maintain a pen-pal network and have more than 400,000 members worldwide. Write them at 380 Riverside Drive, New York, NY 10025. The phone number is (212) 662-2327.

335 Sponsor a hunger banquet. Raise awareness of the world's hunger problem the way a group called Oxfam America does it. Their hunger banquets invite guests who have no idea what they'll be fed. When they arrive, a small group of guests gets a typical American meal. A much larger group gets the bare essentials of rice and beans. An even larger group—more than half—gets a diet lacking in essential food value. Picture the party guests as representing everyone in the world, and you'll get an idea of how many people go hungry while a few get all they want. Oxfam America, 26 West Street, Boston, MA 02111-1206.

336 Fill friendship boxes for the Red Cross.

For needy children in other countries, the Red Cross has special boxes you can fill with little gifts, crayons and coloring books, and small toys. At holiday time, you can add cards and special greetings. The boxes come in handy when there has been a disaster somewhere in the world or right here at home. Contact your regional or local Red Cross chapter for the empty boxes.

337 Adopt a marine squadron. During the Persian Gulf war, the kids of Bonita Canyon Elementary School in Irvine, California, became pen pals with soldiers in the Middle East and helped their

families back home by collecting gifts, sports equipment, and food. They also sponsored a holiday party for the soldiers' loved ones.

And Here Are
Some More:

338 Form a junior United Nations.

339 Start a political club.

340 Start a foreign language club.

341 Send educational supplies to kids in other countries.

342 Write letters to world leaders (including our own) about things that concern you.

HOW TO MAKE YOUR PENNIES AND DOLLARS HELP

RAISING FUNDS TO MAKE A DIFFERENCE.

You've scrubbed, visited, worked, and shown your concern. You've given your time, your energy, and your ideas. And still you wonder, what more can I do?

Sometimes, the only way to improve a particular problem is to raise money. Fund raising can be an important and rewarding activity; there's nothing like watching the total climb as you approach your goal.

And you can be incredibly creative about how you do it. For instance, have you ever heard of Meadow Muffin Bingo? It's a fund-raising event used by the town athletics fund in Hanover, Massachusetts, and sponsored by the 4-H. A 4-H member, Corinna Schembari, describes how it works.

"Basically, the organization sponsoring it secures a large field and marks if off into equal squares. Then they sell 'deeds' to these squares. On the day of the event, they fence in the field and turn a cow or cows out there. Then, whichever square the cow relieves itself in is the winner!'' The winner typically gets about half the money, and the rest goes to charity.

Another group of kids sponsored a rabbit-jumping contest to raise money to save the rainforest. The rabbits never really jumped, but everyone had a great time laughing at the animals and the kids put together a nice pot of money.

Charity fund drives can bring out the best in your group, because they get a lot of people involved. But there's a right way and a wrong way to go about it. Collecting money can be dangerous, and you want to make sure you stay safe. Here are some tips you should follow.

1. Work with supervision from an adult.
Unless you are accustomed to handling lots of money, it's very easy to lose or misplace what you collect. Another problem is, there are people out there who would love to take it away from you. Your parents or a friend's parents can wait out in the car, but if you are going door to door to collect money, they should be close by you.

2. Identify yourself.
If your group has ID cards or a uniform, such as a scout uniform, you should wear it. Also, put the logo or name of the group that will be receiving the money on the container you are using for collection. If the group has canisters or boxes for you to use (such as

UNICEF trick-or-treat canisters) you should always use them.

3. Let them know the purpose of the charity.
Make your statement brief. If the organization has flyers or other literature that describe its activities, you should carry some to leave with the people you are asking for money.

4. Tell them how the money will be spent.
Different charities work different ways. Sometimes all of the money goes to the people the charity is designed to help. Sometimes part of the money is used to fund the group's activities or pay for newsletters and mailings. If you are sending the money to another group to spend, try to find out from them how much of the money actually goes where you want it to go. You may be surprised to find many groups take a big bite out of your dollar just to keep the organization going.

5. Be prepared to give a receipt.
Most people won't ask for one when you are collecting change or small bills, but if someone asks for a slip of paper proving they gave you money, you should be prepared to give them one. The receipt needs to be signed and dated, with the amount of the contribution clearly written out. And it should include the name or logo of your group.

6. Be polite.
It can be frustrating when someone turns you down, but remember there are all sorts of charities in the

world and the person who refuses to support yours
probably gives money to another one.

7. Always keep the money separate.
Don't just stuff it in the same pocket with your spending money, even if you think you'll remember which
is which. After a long day and a few stops for snacks,
you'll never be able to remember. Use a special enve-
lope or a box or a jar or can with an opening in the
top. If you can prepare it in a way that shows it won't
be opened—say, with tape around the lid—people
will feel more comfortable about putting their money
through the slot.

**8. Give the money to an adult who can write a check to
the charity.**
It's never safe to send cash through the mail, where
it must pass through many hands and can get lost
or stolen.

Try one of these activities, or come up with one of
your own.

343 Make handcrafts. Paint T-shirts, make
homemade paper, or knit scarves to sell.

344 Bake up a storm. Get out your best recipes
for cookies, cupcakes, cakes, or bread.

345 Sell flowers or vegetables. Turn the garden into a charity money maker.

346 **H**ave a **walk-a-thon.** Or a swim-a-thon, bike-a-thon, trike-a-thon, dance-a-thon, rake-a-thon, or jump-rope-a-thon. Anything that can get a lot of people together can be a great event. The way it works is, you get friends and relatives to pledge a certain amount of money for every mile, or lap, or hour, or garbage bag full of leaves, or number of times you jump. Can you think of any other "a-thons" to try?

347 **H**ave a **car wash.** Wear old clothes. For some reason, everybody always seems to get a little bit wet at these things!

348 **G**ive a **yard sale.** Get rid of the junk your family doesn't need and turn it into cash for your chosen charity.

349 **S**hovel snow. It's great exercise and a good way to show people you really care about the group you are helping.

350 **M**ake a **haunted house in your gym.** At Halloween time, decorate the gym as a creepy and weird place and charge money to scare the daylights out of people.

351 **R**ent your **service club.** Publicize that your club will do whatever people need doing for a day, or for a month of Saturdays, and charge them for your services.

352 **H**ave a carnival. Fill your yard with games, tell fortunes, have pony rides.

353 **C**ook up a pasta-eating contest.

354 **H**old a raffle. People pay to take a chance on winning something valuable. Often, businesses will donate the gifts in return for the publicity. Be careful—some states don't allow raffles, or have laws that restrict them.

355 **F**ire away with a charity barbecue. (Supervised, of course!)

356 **C**hallenge the adults to a charity baseball game. Only they have to play wronghanded!

357 **P**ut on a talent show.

358 **G**et people to buy a chance at guessing the number of beans or candies in a giant jar.

359 Have a charity trivia contest.

360 Walk dogs for charity.

361 Hold a penny harvest. Pennies buy so little most people consider them a waste of time. But if you collect them from everyone in your apartment building or where your parents work that could be quite a lot.

362 Open a lemonade stand.

363 Have a charity animal fair with all your friends, with ribbons for best animals in the show.

364 Have an art show and sale.

THe FiNAL
WAY TO HeLP

HELP US THINK OF MORE WAYS!

Can you believe it? No matter how hard we tried, we couldn't come up with number 365. We need your help.

We want you to write to Nickelodeon and tell us how you share, clean, fix, care, give, or do. It doesn't have to be a long or involved account. Just tell us in your own words what you've done in the spirit of volunteering your time, your generosity, your strength or your ideas.

365 HELP! Write to:
Nickelodeon
P.O. Box 2626
New York, NY 10108

Make sure you include your name, age, address, and phone number. If we do another edition of this book, we want to include your help project in it!

Nickelodeon has joined forces with a number of organizations to help match you up with a volunteer project. You can write or call them for information on volunteer opportunities in your area. Mention that you heard about them from The Big Help on "Nickelodeon."

Youth Service America, 1101 15th Street NW, Suite 200, Washington, DC 20005; (202) 296-2992. YSA has over 200 national affiliated youth programs around the country and over 5,000 local programs. The organization is a leader in the national and community service field.

Points of Light Foundation, 1737 H Street NW, Washington, DC 20006; (202) 223-9186. POL works in partnership with over 600 volunteer centers around the country. The aim is to solve the most serious social problems in the world today through community service.

Second Harvest, 116 South Michigan Avenue, Chicago, IL 60603-6001; (800) 532-FOOD. A nationwide network of 185 food banks that supply food to nearly 50,000 local charitable agencies. Each year, more than 500 million pounds of food from Second Harvest suppliers feed the needy in all fifty states.

National 4-H, 14th Street and Independence SW, Ag Box 0904, Washington, DC 20250; (202) 720-5853. With over 3,100 programs around the country, 4-H is a world leader in making positive change in society.

Earth Force, 1501 Wilson Boulevard, Arlington, VA 22209; (703) 243-7400. A national organization inspired by young people to sponsor environmental education, environmental action, and public citizenship.

About the Author

Alan Goodman was part of the creative team that developed the modern Nickelodeon network and made it the #1 Network for Kids. As a producer, he was a co-creator and executive producer of Kids Court, which won many awards from educational associations and an award from Action for Children's Television; he co-created, produced, and wrote the Kids' Choice Awards specials; he was co-producer and head writer of "Clarissa Explains It All;" and was head writer of "Hey Dude."

Before his work with Nickelodeon, he was one of the people who developed MTV, and has won many awards for animation and shows on the channel. He has also written and produced shows for CBS, PBS, Cinemax, The Movie Channel, and Comedy Central.

*"If nobody did anything, nothing in the world would be different.
Not everyone realizes that kids can make a difference too.
Some adults think we can't, but we can."*
— 9 year-old girl, talking about volunteering

Help your community!

Get in on the action!

Kids can make a big difference! Nickelodeon's The Big Help campaign gives you the opportunity to help in your community.

- **THE BIG HELP™ Book**, by Alan Goodman: Hundreds of ways—big and small—that you can help. Available wherever books are sold.

- **THE BIG HELP™ Telethon**: This fall, Nickelodeon will air a telethon that asks you and kids across the country to call in and pledge time, not money. Then you can spend the amount of time you pledged helping others.

- **THE BIG HELP™ Day**: A national celebration for kids, parents, and everyone else who participates in THE BIG HELP™

Why Nickelodeon? Nick believes that kids deserve to have their voices heard and their questions answered. Through events like 1992's Kids Pick the President, 1993's Kids World Council: Plan It for the Planet, and now the THE BIG HELP™, Nick strives to connect kids to each other and the world.

A MINSTREL BOOK